The Crown of Kuros

An allegory
by Ed Dunlop

(BOOK FOUR IN THE TERRESTRIA CHRONICLES)

And that he died for all,

that they which live should not

henceforth live unto themselves,

but unto him which died for them,

and rose again.

– II Corinthians 5:15

Books by Ed Dunlop

The Terrestria Chronicles
The Sword, the Ring, and the Parchment
The Quest for Seven Castles
The Search for Everyman
The Crown of Kuros
The Dragon's Egg
The Golden Lamps
The Great War

Jed Cartwright Adventure Series
The Midnight Escape
The Lost Gold Mine
The Comanche Raiders
The Lighthouse Mystery
The Desperate Slave
The Midnight Rustlers

The Young Refugees Series
Escape to Liechtenstein
The Search for the Silver Eagle
The Incredible Rescues

Sherlock Jones Detective Series
Sherlock Jones and the Assassination Plot
Sherlock Jones and the Willoughby Bank Robbery
Sherlock Jones and the Missing Diamond
Sherlock Jones and the Phantom Airplane
Sherlock Jones and the Hidden Coins
Sherlock Jones and the Odyssey Mystery

The 1,000-Mile Journey

Christian fiction: Ages 10 and up
www.dunlopministries.com
Cover Art by Laura Lea Sencabaugh and Wayne Coley

That my heart might be

yielded to my King

Chapter One

The tall archer reached over his left shoulder and snatched an arrow from his quiver. In one smooth, fluid motion, he nocked the arrow on the string of his longbow and drew the bowstring back until the feathers of the fletching touched his right cheek. The muscles in his brawny arms stood out as he held the position, standing at full draw for the briefest instant before releasing the arrow. At the sharp twang of the bowstring, the arrow leaped from the archer's bow. It sped through the air with a blur of motion so swift that the eye could not follow. In an instant, the arrowhead had buried itself deeply in the stiff woven straw mat of the target.

Prince Selwyn groaned. "Another bull's-eye! Sir Pretentious has another bull's-eye!"

"Aye, but I hope he doesn't win," his sister, Princess Gilda, replied. "Sir Pretentious is so proud and arrogant! If he wins the archery tournament, he'll be even more boastful than ever. I hope Sir Humility wins."

Selwyn glanced across the meadow to the spot where Sir Pretentious' quiet rival stood calmly in the shade of a tall sycamore that was losing its leaves. "Sir Humility doesn't seem worried."

At that moment, a splendid milk-white charger came dashing along the approach to the Castle of Faith. The rider, a young prince wearing the armor and colors of King Emmanuel, leaned low in the saddle and urged his mount to greater speed. The magnificent horse left the roadway and thundered across the grassy meadow toward the colorful tents that marked the entrance to the tournament. Moments later the horse slowed to a canter as he reached the edge of the crowd of eager spectators. The prince reined to a stop beside Selwyn and Gilda. Dismounting quickly, he lifted the visor of his helmet, revealing a lock of dark hair and a pleasant face with lively brown eyes. "How is the tournament going?" he asked eagerly.

"Josiah," Selwyn greeted him in a way that told that the two were good friends, "where have you been?"

The young prince let out a sigh. "I've been on a trifling quest for Sir Faithful," he replied, gazing at the targets in the distance where tournament officials were validating and recording the archers' scores. "I had to ride to the Castle of Assurance to pick up some parchments." He looked hopefully from Gilda to Selwyn. "Who's winning?"

"Eighty paces!" an official called. "Move the targets to eighty paces!"

"There are only twelve archers left in the tournament," Selwyn told Josiah. "Right now, Sir Pretentious, Sir Humility, Sir Constant and Sir Peaceable are all tied for first place."

"We're hoping that Sir Humility will win," Gilda added.

Josiah smiled at her. "He's one of the best archers in all of Terrestria." He turned to Selwyn. "How did you do?"

Selwyn shrugged. "Not too well. I was eliminated in the second round."

Josiah frowned. "I wish I could have been here to compete," he complained. "I wouldn't have won, but I'm sure that I could have placed well." He grimaced. "Instead, I got stuck running an errand for Sir Faithful that any servant in the castle could have done."

"The contestants will now shoot at the mark from a distance of eighty paces," a herald announced. "Each will shoot a dozen arrows. The winners of this round will compete in the final round of the tournament!"

The twelve archers stepped forward with their longbows in their left hands. A hush fell over the crowd of spectators.

Josiah felt a tug at his sleeve and turned to see a young page looking timidly up at him. "Sire, Sir Faithful sent me to fetch you," the boy told the young prince. "He's waiting in his solar and he needs to see you immediately."

Josiah nodded impatiently as he glanced up at the white marble walls of the Castle of Faith. *I've already missed most of the tournament,* he thought resentfully. *I don't want to miss the conclusion.* "I'll be there in just a minute," he told the boy. The page nodded and moved away, and the young prince turned his attention back to the archers.

"Sir Humility, advance to the mark," an official called. "You may fire when ready."

The archer stepped forward, drawing an arrow from his quiver as he did. Nocking the arrow, he pulled the bowstring back to a full draw and held it for an instant. The crowd waited breathlessly. With the twang of the bowstring the arrow sped from

Sir Humility's bow to strike the target just above the bull's-eye. Josiah winced.

"Sir Pretentious, advance to the mark and fire when ready," the official called.

The arrogant archer took his place with a confident smile on his rugged face. Glancing smugly across the crowd of spectators, he nocked an arrow and almost instantly sent it flying toward his target. The arrow struck the bull's-eye dead center, and a loud groan went up from the spectators. Clearly, they were not hoping for a win for Sir Pretentious. The archer's lip curled in anger as he flashed them a look of irritation.

Josiah, Selwyn, and Gilda watched anxiously as the tournament continued. By the time each archer had fired his third arrow, it had become obvious that this round would eliminate all but Sir Pretentious, Sir Humility, Sir Constant, and Sir Peaceable. These four outstanding archers would compete in the final round of the tournament. Sir Humility had just stepped to the mark to fire his fourth arrow when Josiah felt a tug at his sleeve. He turned to find the page who had delivered the message from Sir Faithful just moments before.

"Sir Faithful is waiting, my lord," the young boy said respectfully. "He really needs to see you, sire!"

"Thank you, page," Josiah replied casually. "I will come shortly."

"But he needs to see you now, sire."

"I said that I'll come," Josiah replied impatiently, flicking the reins in his hand to show his irritation. "I'll be there in just a moment." He gave the page a fierce look and the boy hurried away without further words.

Josiah turned just in time to see Sir Humility's arrow strike the target for a perfect bull's-eye. "Do you know what Sir Faithful wants?" Selwyn asked him.

"He just wants the parchments that I brought back from the Castle of Assurance," Josiah replied with a nonchalant shrug. "I'll take them to him in a minute."

"Shouldn't you go now?" Gilda suggested, with an earnest look in her clear blue eyes.

Josiah watched an archer step up to the mark, fitting an arrow to the string of his longbow as he did. "I'll go in just a minute," he repeated, without looking at Gilda or Selwyn. "I don't want to miss the rest of the tournament."

Within minutes the field of archers had been narrowed to the four favored competitors. "The targets will now be moved to a distance of one hundred paces," an official barked. "The winner of this round is the champion of the entire tournament!"

A thrill of anticipation swept across the crowd of eager spectators and they began to chatter excitedly as the targets were moved down the field to the specified distance. Josiah took a deep breath. "Sir Humility has to win this round," he told his companions. "He has to!" Josiah's horse nuzzled his shoulder as if to show that he was in complete agreement with the young prince.

"Sire, Sir Faithful has to see you. He has to see you *now!*"

Josiah glanced at the persistent page and let out a sigh of frustration. "All right, all right," he retorted irritably. "I'll go! But you must tend to my horse." Dropping the reins, the young prince reached for his saddlebags and pulled out three rolled parchments. "I really don't see why it's so important that I go right now," he muttered under his breath. "I'm going to miss the rest of the tournament!"

Prince Josiah strode angrily across the meadow and hurried up the steep approach to the Castle of Faith. As he stomped across the drawbridge, the sound of his sabotons on the timbers echoed in the moat. His spurs rattled and jingled with every angry step. *I'm going to miss the rest of the tournament,* he fretted. *Why couldn't Sir Faithful have waited just another few minutes? By the time I get back to the tournament, it will all be over!* The sentries at the gate saluted him as he entered the gatehouse, but he didn't notice.

Clutching the parchments in his left hand, Josiah took the stairs two at a time. He hurried into Sir Faithful's solar without taking the time to knock. The elderly castle steward was seated at his desk, and he looked up as the young prince entered. "Here, sire," Josiah said hurriedly, placing the parchments on the old man's desk. "The documents from the Castle of Assurance." He turned to leave.

The old man clutched at his arm. "Josiah, my prince, what is your hurry?"

Josiah paused and forced a smile. "Was there something else, sire?"

"How did the journey go, my son?"

Josiah shrugged. "It was uneventful, sire. I encountered no opposition from Argamor's men." He stood quietly, anxious to get away, trying to quell his impatience at being delayed. He was missing the archery tournament and this was no time to be exchanging pleasantries.

If Sir Faithful sensed his impatience, he showed so sign of it.

"And how did you find matters at the Castle of Assurance, lad?"

"Things seemed to be going well, sire." He gestured toward the parchments. "You will find the records that you were wanting right there, sire." He edged toward the door.

The old man picked up the parchments and thrust them into Josiah's hands. "Come with me, lad. Carry them down to the keep for me." He turned and picked up a basket piled high with similar parchments, and Josiah vented his emotions in a long sigh of frustration.

I want to see Sir Humility compete against Sir Pretentious, he told himself with a rising sense of helpless anger. *But if Sir Faithful keeps me busy running errands for him, I'm going to miss the entire tournament!* Biting his lip, he followed the castle steward through the door.

Sir Faithful led him down several flights of stairs into the very heart of the castle. Together the old man and the youth passed through a musty corridor and approached a dark archway that Josiah had never seen before. Peering into the blackness beyond the archway, Josiah saw a shadowy tunnel. Two armed guards, one on each side of the entryway, bowed to Sir Faithful and Prince Josiah as they approached. One of them handed a flickering lamp to Sir Faithful while the other took a ring of keys from the steward, hurried into the tunnel, and unlocked a massive iron door at the other end. A moment later he handed the keys back to Sir Faithful.

The steward and the prince entered the tunnel, stepped through the doorway, and entered a large room with a low ceiling. Josiah held his breath and stared about the room in awe. The flickering flame of the lamp illuminated glittering stores of treasure. A line of huge wooden chests against one wall held gleaming piles of golden coins; the opposite wall held shelf after shelf of smaller chests filled with sparkling diamonds, rubies, emeralds, sapphires and pearls. The far end of the treasure vault was piled high with large bars of gold and silver. Row after row of pigeonhole compartments on the wall above the cache of gold and silver ingots held scores of rolled parchments.

"Sire, what is this place?" Josiah asked breathlessly.

"This is King Emmanuel's treasure vault, known as the keep," Sir Faithful replied. "It is the most secure place in the castle. Only Sir Watchful and I have keys to it. He and I handpicked a special detachment of guards to keep watch over it night and day. We maintain such tight security because the crown jewels are kept here, as well as the royal treasure and the important records of the kingdom."

As Prince Josiah watched, the steward placed the basket of parchments on the floor. Taking them one by one from the basket, he carefully placed the parchments in their proper places in the wooden cubbyholes. He then took the three documents that Josiah carried and placed them with care in the compartments. The old man had not yet dismissed him, so the young prince waited impatiently. *Hurry*, he urged silently. *Please hurry!* When the last of the parchments was in place, Sir Faithful then chose others from the wall and placed them with great care in the basket.

"We are finished here," the castle steward said, handing the lamp to Josiah and using both hands to pick the basket up from the floor. Josiah heaved a sigh of relief but Sir Faithful didn't seem to notice. "You may return to the archery tournament," he said quietly, and Josiah looked at him quickly, surprised that the old man knew the cause of his impatience. "But first, lock the door of the keep behind me."

"How do I do that, sire?" Josiah asked.

"Just push the door shut and pull the handle down," Sir Faithful replied, moving toward the entrance to the vault. "The door will lock." He hurried away, leaving the young prince standing alone at the massive door.

Prince Josiah reached out and pushed against the iron door with one hand. The massive barrier refused to move. Setting the lamp on the floor, the young prince placed both hands high on the door and leaned against it with all his strength. With a creak of protesting hinges, the huge door began to move—slowly at first and then faster and faster until it clanged shut. Josiah reached for the handle.

Just then a distant noise reached the ears of the young prince. He paused, listening intently, and his eyes widened in dismay. Even though he was deep within the heart of the Castle of Faith, he could hear the sounds of a wildly cheering crowd. His heart sank. The tournament! Something crucial had just taken place at the archery tournament, and he had missed it!

Snatching the lamp from the floor, he hurried from the tunnel, handing the lamp to the guards as he passed. Knowing in his heart that he was too late to witness the tournament's conclusion, he nevertheless retraced his steps as fast as he could. He ran at full speed down the corridor. As he reached the stairs, the noise of the cheering crowd increased. Josiah took the stairs two at a time, completely unaware that his impatience had just created an incident that would impact the entire kingdom of Terrestria.

Chapter Two

Prince Josiah dashed through the main gate of the Castle of Faith, across the drawbridge, and down the embankment toward the meadow where the archery tournament was being held. As he ran toward the event, he was dismayed to see the noisy crowd of spectators making their way toward him. He stopped and gritted his teeth in anger. The tournament was over! He had missed it!

"If Sir Faithful had waited just a few minutes," he snarled to no one in particular, "I could have seen the conclusion. But no, he had to have the parchments right then, and so I missed the most exciting part of the tournament!" Overcome with frustration and anger at what he perceived as a great injustice, he clenched his fists.

"Josiah! You should have seen it!" Princess Gilda hurried toward him, her eyes shining with excitement. Her brother was right behind her. "Sir Humility and Sir Pretentious were tied right till the very end," the girl went on, waving her hands in delight. "They both had to shoot from one hundred and twenty paces to break the tie, and Sir Humility won. It was the most exciting thing I've ever seen!"

"Aye, well I'm glad that you enjoyed it," Josiah growled bitterly. "I was too busy running errands to see any of it."

Selwyn looked at him quizzically, but said nothing.

"Sir Humility got three bull's-eyes from that distance, but Sir Pretentious only got two!" Gilda gushed, oblivious to the young prince's foul mood. "The whole crowd cheered and cheered, and that made Sir Pretentious angry. He stalked from the field before the officials even had a chance to proclaim Sir Humility as champion. Tonight they're going to present Sir Humility with the—"

Josiah cut her off. "I have heard enough, Gilda. Speak no more about it!" He turned and walked toward the castle.

The young prince and princess fell in step beside Josiah. Gilda glanced up at Josiah's angry face. She said nothing, but her eyes mirrored her hurt feelings.

That night the great hall of the Castle of Faith buzzed with excitement as the residents gathered for the evening meal. Knights and their ladies strolled casually into the huge hall, laughing and conversing warmly with each other. Squires and pages called to each other, and children laughed and chattered happily. Ladies-in-waiting exchanged greetings with members of the castle staff while servants and scullions hurried here and there, filling goblets and bearing platters of food. A minstrel stood in one corner, frowning in concentration as he tuned the strings on his lute. In the noisy hustle and bustle of the preparation for the evening meal, the atmosphere in the great hall was one of anticipation, happiness and contentment.

Prince Josiah walked to the King's table, which enjoyed a place of prominence in the spacious great hall, and took a seat. Prince Selwyn and Princess Gilda soon joined him. The young prince looked wistfully at the empty chair at the head of the table. If only King Emmanuel would return soon from the Golden City!

Moments later, Sir Faithful made his way to the table, accompanied by Sir Watchful, the castle constable. A host of servants swarmed about the tables bearing platters piled high with tempting food. After sending a petition of thanksgiving, the residents of the castle were soon enjoying miniature meat pastries, pheasant in cinnamon sauce, beef fritters, eels in spicy puree, loaches in cold green sauce, slices of roast mutton, filets of saltwater fish, and various garden vegetables.

The meal had barely started when a castle guard came rushing into the great hall. Josiah took one look at the man's face and knew that something dreadful had happened. The guard hurried to the King's table. Leaning close to Sir Faithful, he whispered an urgent message in the old man's ear. Sir Faithful's hands flew to his long, white beard and a look of distress crossed his face. Without a word to those around the table, he jumped to his feet and hurried from the great hall with the guard close on his heels. Sir Watchful rose and hurried after them.

Selwyn leaned over to Josiah. "What do you think has happened?" he whispered.

"Nay, I know not," Josiah replied quietly, "but from the look on Sir Faithful's face I would say that something dreadful has occurred." He thought for a moment. "Perhaps Argamor has attacked one of the castles again."

Gilda overheard him. "I hope not," she whispered.

Josiah looked up to realize that a hush had fallen over the great hall. The minstrel had stopped playing. The lords and ladies sat silent. Even the servants and scullions stood still—many of them bearing platters of food—as if they were afraid to break the silence. Every eye was turned toward Sir Faithful's empty chair, and the young prince realized that the entire assembly had witnessed the steward's hasty exit. The anxious looks on the faces of the lords and ladies told him that he was right—something was amiss in the Castle of Faith.

Food was forgotten as the residents of the castle waited anxiously for the steward's return. Tension filled the great hall. Obviously, the lords and ladies of the King's court were worried. The atmosphere reminded Josiah of the eerie silence that often precedes a violent thunderstorm. He shivered as a cold chill crept up his back. An indescribable feeling of uneasiness swept over him.

After several moments of silence, the minstrel began to play softly. He did not sing; he simply strummed the strings of his lute and a gentle melody wafted across the great hall. Josiah immediately saw the effects of the soothing music: the lords and ladies relaxed visibly and began to whisper quietly to one another.

Josiah glanced over at Gilda and saw that her eyes were wide. He smiled at her, and she smiled back.

The minstrel suddenly stopped playing. All eyes went immediately to the enormous door of the great hall. Sir Faithful stood framed in the doorway.

As the lords and ladies, servants and scullions, pages and squires and knights all watched in silence, the castle steward walked slowly to the far end of the great hall. His face was lined with worry. His head was bowed as he ascended the steps of the dais and stood beside King Emmanuel's empty throne. He cleared his throat. The silence in the great hall was overwhelming.

Josiah waited anxiously. Something was wrong, dreadfully so, but what could it be?

Sir Faithful nervously stroked his beard as his gaze swept across the breathless castle residents. He cleared his throat a second time, and then began to speak. "My beloved friends, the moment has come that I have long feared. I regret that I must be the one to bring such dreadful news." The elderly steward was speaking in a soft, sorrowful voice, but his words carried easily across the vast great hall. He swallowed hard, and Josiah saw an expression of pain and regret in his kind eyes.

"It brings me great sorrow to tell you this, my friends, but the Crown of Kuros has disappeared from the Castle of Faith. It was taken from King Emmanuel's treasure vault sometime today."

Exclamations of dismay and disbelief echoed across the vastness of the great hall. Josiah had never heard of the Crown of Kuros, but the responses that greeted Sir Faithful's announcement told the young prince that the loss was a great one. After the initial reaction of distress, the castle residents sat in stunned silence. No one moved. It was as if time itself were standing still.

"We do not know how the crown could possibly have disappeared, but the fact remains—its place in the vault is empty. I have already asked Sir Watchful to secure the castle gate; no one will go in or out until we have searched the entire castle. My friends, I do not need to remind you of the seriousness of the situation. The Crown of Kuros must not fall into the hands of Argamor."

Chapter Three

Prince Josiah shuddered at Sir Faithful's words. The mere mention of Argamor's name brought back painful memories. Argamor, a skilled musician who had once served in King Emmanuel's court in the Golden City of the Redeemed, was now the sworn enemy of the King. It had happened so long ago that no one could remember exactly when it was, but Argamor had attempted to lead a revolt against His Majesty, King Emmanuel. When the revolt failed, Argamor had been exiled from the Golden City. Even now it was rumored that he was making plans to attempt to seize King Emmanuel's throne.

The young prince shuddered again as he thought of his years of cruel servitude to Argamor. For a time, Argamor had worked as a blacksmith in the Village of Despair, making chains of slavery for the people of Terrestria. Josiah had served as his slave, spending his days hauling coal for his master's forge and spending his nights in the Dungeon of Condemnation. Nearly a year and a half had passed since King Emmanuel had come in the Coach of Grace and freed the boy from Argamor's cruelty. Feelings of love and gratitude swept across Josiah's soul as he recalled that blessed day when the mighty King had adopted him into the royal family.

"The Crown of Kuros must not fall into Argamor's hands!" Sir Faithful said again, raising his voice and lifting his hands for emphasis. "We must search the kingdom until we find it!"

Josiah leaned over to Selwyn. "What is the Crown of Kuros?" he asked in a whisper. "I have never heard of it."

"Of a truth, I'm not sure," his friend replied quietly.

"The Crown of Kuros is the most precious of the crown jewels, sires," a knight at a nearby table told them softly, leaning toward them as he spoke. "The word *kuros* is an ancient word meaning *supremacy*. The Crown of Kuros is actually the symbol of King Emmanuel's supremacy over Terrestria; it is the token of his right to the throne."

Josiah's mind raced. "So if the crown fell into someone else's hands, that person would have the right to rule Terrestria, instead of King Emmanuel?"

The knight nodded soberly. "So it would seem, sire. That is why the crown must never fall into Argamor's hands."

Argamor ruling Terrestria. The very thought made Josiah shudder.

"Captain Diligence and Captain Assurance."

As Sir Faithful called the names of the two commanders of the castle garrisons, both stalwart knights stood to their feet. "At your service, sire."

"Leave your sentries in place atop the castle walls and gates, but put together a detail of the rest of your men and have them search the Castle of Faith from top to bottom. Search every solar, every courtyard and corridor, every nook and cranny of the kitchen and armory and stables. Look in the well. Leave no stone unturned. If the Crown of Kuros is still within the castle walls, I want it found tonight."

"Aye, sire," both commanders responded.

"And another thing," the castle steward continued, "have Sir Memory and Sir Devotion sent here immediately. Unless I am mistaken, they were the guards on duty at the keep when the crown was taken."

"Aye, sire."

Moments later the two guards were standing nervously before the castle steward. A profound silence reigned in the great hall. Dinner was forgotten.

"As you have just learned," Sir Faithful said, addressing Sir Memory and Sir Devotion, "the Crown of Kuros was taken from King Emmanuel's vault. The crown was in its proper place when Prince Josiah and I visited the vault this morning, so it had to have been stolen sometime today. Did anyone else attempt to approach the vault after the prince and I visited it this morning?"

Both men shook their heads. "Nay, sire," Sir Devotion replied. "Just you, sire."

"I'm talking about the period of time after the visit that the prince and I made to the vault. Are you certain that no one else came near the vault?"

"Just you, sire," the guard repeated. "You were the only one who visited the King's treasure vault this afternoon."

Sir Faithful's mouth dropped open. "But I did not visit the keep this afternoon."

A puzzled look appeared on Sir Devotion's face. "Aye, but you did, sire. You came to the vault to return a few parchments. Sir Memory and I distinctly remember it." The other guard nodded in agreement.

The castle steward was trembling. "Sires, tell everything that you remember about this second visit to King Emmanuel's vault."

Sir Memory spoke up. "You came to the keep about three o'clock this afternoon, sire. You had three parchments that you were returning—"

"Four," Sir Devotion interrupted. "He was carrying four parchments."

"Three or four—I don't suppose that it matters," Sir Faithful said, looking from one guard to the other. "Pray, continue with your account."

"Aye. When you approached the keep, I asked for your key, but you replied that you would rather unlock it yourself," Sir Memory continued. "It seemed a bit unusual, but you unlocked the vault by yourself and entered. You deposited the parchments and left the vault rather hurriedly. When we found the vault door unlocked just moments ago, we sent Sir Concern to notify you immediately. We were not aware that the crown had been taken."

For a moment, silence reigned in the great hall. The tension was so great that Josiah found it difficult to breathe.

"And you're certain that I was this second visitor to the keep?" the steward questioned.

"It looked like you, sire," Sir Devotion replied, "and it sounded like you. Neither of us had any doubt that it was you. The only thing we noticed out of the ordinary was the fact that you insisted on unlocking the door by yourself instead of giving us your key and allowing us to do it for you."

The great hall was silent as Sir Faithful pondered the information. "An impostor has done this," he said slowly. "Someone has entered the castle impersonating me, somehow gained entrance to the keep, and stolen the Crown of Kuros!"

A murmur of bewilderment swept across the great hall.

"But, sire, it seemed to be you," Sir Memory said. "Whoever it was that entered the vault was able to imitate your voice perfectly!"

Sir Watchful entered the great hall just then. "The main gate and the postern gate are both secured, Sir Faithful. No one will leave the castle until I say so." He approached the dais upon which the castle steward stood. "I heard you speak of an impostor in the castle. My men told me of a crippled beggar who entered the main gate this morning, but no one has seen him since. Perhaps—"

"Morphina!" As Sir Faithful said the name, a rumble of indignation swept across the great hall.

Josiah turned to the knight at the next table. "Sire, I have never heard of Morphina. Who is he?"

"She," the knight corrected. "Morphina is an evil enchantress who has the power to change her appearance as rapidly as does a chameleon. She can even take on the appearance of another person. She is in league with Argamor. If Morphina is the one who has stolen the Crown of Kuros, the kingdom of Terrestria is indeed in jeopardy!"

"Dispatch a message to the Golden City," Sir Faithful told Sir Watchful. "Ask His Majesty to send his armies to search the kingdom for this wicked enchantress. She must be found before she delivers the crown to Argamor!"

The castle constable nodded in agreement and strode quickly from the great hall.

A knight approached Sir Faithful. "Sire," he said, "even if Morphina could use her power of disguise to gain access to the castle, she would not be able to unlock the door of the vault. Only you and Sir Watchful have the keys. How could she have gained access to the Crown of Kuros unless she had the keys?"

Sir Faithful thought about that for a moment. He raised his eyes and beckoned to Josiah. "Come hither, my prince."

Josiah's heart was in his throat as he approached the dais. "Aye, sire?"

"Prince Josiah, did you indeed close the door to King Emmanuel's vault this morning when I asked you to? Did you lock it?"

Josiah's heart pounded. His hands shook as he answered, "Aye, sire, I was careful to lock the door as you instructed."

"Are you certain, my prince?"

Josiah paused for just a moment, trying to remember just what had taken place as he left the treasure vault. In his imagination he could see the enormous door, so massive, so heavy... "Aye," he replied, a bit more certain now. "I remember that the door was much heavier than I had imagined. I tried to close it with one hand, but found that I could not. I had to set the lamp on the floor so that I could use both hands to close it. I'm certain, sire."

Sir Faithful nodded. "That's all that I need to know." He

smiled at the young prince. "I just wanted to be sure that you are certain, Josiah. Morphina could not have gotten into the keep without help from someone within the castle."

Josiah let out a sigh of relief as he returned to his seat. His thoughts were in turmoil. *The Crown of Kuros has been taken! How could Morphina have gotten into the Castle of Faith, and especially, into the keep where King Emmanuel's treasure and records were kept? I wonder who was responsible for letting her in.*

He caught his breath as a horrible idea suddenly occurred to him. *What if I didn't lock the door of the keep properly? What if I am the one who allowed the wicked Morphina to enter King Emmanuel's treasure vault and steal the Crown of Kuros?* The thought troubled him and was almost more than he could bear.

Josiah shook his head as if to clear his mind of such bothersome thoughts. *I locked it,* he told himself firmly. *I know I did! Sir Faithful asked me to, and I can still remember pushing that heavy, heavy door closed. It made a weighty clanging noise when it shut. I remember.*

"*But did you lock it?*" a nagging voice inside seemed to whisper. "*You closed it, but did you lock it? Perchance you are the one who allowed Morphina to enter the keep. The Crown of Kuros is missing. Perchance this disaster is all your fault.*" Josiah shook his head vehemently and covered his ears with his hands as if to shut out the accusing voice. Selwyn was watching him with a strange expression on his face, but Josiah didn't notice.

I closed the door, Josiah argued. *I locked it. I know that I did! I am not the one who allowed Morphina to enter the keep and steal the Crown of Kuros. I had nothing to do with that.*

"*Did you lock it?*" the voice asked, accusingly. "*You closed the door to the vault, but did you lock it?"*

"Aye," Josiah said aloud. "I locked it!"

Selwyn leaned over. "What's the matter, Josiah?" he asked quietly. "Are you all right?"

The young prince took a deep breath and let it out slowly. He looked around the great hall. Many of the lords and ladies were watching him with puzzled expressions on their faces. "Aye, it's all right," he replied in a low voice. "I'm fine."

Sir Faithful lifted his voice and addressed the castle residents. "My lords and my ladies," he began, and his thin voice echoed across the great hall, "today the enchantress Morphina has dealt a major blow against our Lord and Master, His Majesty, King Emmanuel. By entering the Castle of Faith and somehow gaining entrance to the keep—heavily guarded though it was—she has managed to steal the Crown of Kuros." The elderly steward paused and looked around the great hall. "I need not tell you how important that crown is to His Majesty, and to all Terrestria."

The lords and ladies nodded soberly. A few of the ladies wept openly.

"The crown must be recovered for His Majesty!" Sir Faithful thundered, and the rafters rang with the echo of his voice. Several knights drew their swords and raised them in the air as if to show that they were ready to undertake a quest for their King.

"I need not tell you what Morphina plans to do with the crown," Sir Faithful continued. "She will place it in the hands of His Majesty's sworn enemy, Argamor. We must not allow that to happen!"

A knight approached the dais on which Sir Faithful stood. "Sire, what if the enchantress has already surrendered the crown to Argamor?"

Sir Faithful shook his head. "I do not think that has yet taken place," he replied. "We will know when it happens."

At that moment, two guards hurried into the great hall, escorting a thin, haggard stranger between them. The man looked as if he had been trampled by a team of horses. He swayed from side to side; his face was drawn and tired and his eyes mirrored his exhaustion. Across his shoulder was a battered lute. The two castle guards supported him as if he would tumble to the floor if they released him. Together the trio approached the dais. "What is the meaning of this?" Sir Faithful demanded.

"Sire, this man claims that he has an important message for the castle," one of the guards replied. "He demanded to be brought before you."

"What is your message, minstrel?" the castle steward asked the stranger.

"I have a message for the Castle of Faith," the stranger replied. "I bring news of the Crown of Kuros!" A hush fell across the great hall, a silence so intense that you could have heard a mustard seed drop.

Chapter Four

The lords and ladies of the Castle of Faith sat in stunned silence. Sir Faithful moved closer to King Emmanuel's throne, silently studying the stranger as he did. At last he spoke. "Sire, who are you?" he asked. "And from whence have you news of the Crown of Kuros?"

"My lord, I am a humble minstrel," the stranger answered. "I am called by the name Wanderer. I travel from castle to castle, my lord, singing my songs of the kingdom and delivering bits of news and gossip in exchange for a meal and a place to sleep."

"I have heard of you," the castle steward replied. "Pray, tell your story."

The minstrel sank to his knees on the stone floor. "Forgive me, my lord, but I am faint from my journey. I have traveled hard to deliver the news that I bear."

Sir Faithful summoned the servants. "Bring a chair for our guest," he ordered. "Bring the fruit of the vine, and victuals to restore this man's strength. We will wait while he partakes of our hospitality." In no time the minstrel was seated at a table, quenching his thirst from a tall silver goblet and eating hungrily from a huge platter. The castle residents waited patiently.

As he finished eating, the minstrel seemed to gain strength immediately. He stood to his feet and approached the dais where Sir Faithful waited. "I am ready to tell my story, my lord."

"We await whatever news you can tell us of the fate of the Crown of Kuros," the steward replied.

"As I said, my name is Wanderer, and I have spent my days tramping from castle to castle throughout the kingdom, singing my songs and telling my tales. It is a lonely life, my lord, and yet, a richly rewarding one. I keep my eyes and ears open, and I have learned much. Sometimes it is simply amazing what a troubadour such as myself can learn when—"

"You have news of the Crown of Kuros," Sir Faithful interrupted. "Pray, my good man, share what you know of what has happened to the crown."

"Aye, my lord," Wandered replied, bowing to the steward and then to the court. "Tonight I was in the great hall of the Castle of Compromise, perhaps eighty furlongs from here. The castle's residents are divided in their loyalties, sire, with some loyal to Lord Argamor, and—"

"We know the place. Pray, get to the heart of your tale."

"At once, my lord. As I was saying, tonight I was performing at the Castle of Compromise. I was in the midst of spinning a splendid tale of knights and dragons when the doors to the great hall suddenly flew open with tremendous force. I turned, as did the members of the court, but there was no one there as we had expected. The doorway was empty. At that moment, however, a cold chill seemed to enter the great hall. I experienced overwhelming feelings of fear, of hatred, and of evil. Although we could see no one, we all knew that an evil being of great power had entered the hall. It was a terrifying experience, my lord.

"In an instant, the fires in the fireplaces went out, and just as suddenly, the lamps and candles of the chandeliers were extinguished, plunging the great hall into complete darkness. Never in my life have I been so terrified. Although I could see nothing, I was aware of a dark presence, a personage so wicked and so powerful that the great hall was overwhelmed with evil.

"The sound of a rushing wind filled the hall, and suddenly, a huge, pale horse stood glowing before us in the center of the room. He reared up and slashed the air with his fore hooves. He was fully twenty feet tall, my lord. In the darkness of the great hall, the enormous white horse was truly a sight to behold. His breath hung in the air like a luminous cloud. His eyes were orbs of fire. I, like the others in the court, was terrified."

The minstrel paused, took a sip from a goblet on a nearby table, and then continued. "The colossal horse started changing color, my lord, turning to bay and then golden yellow and then steel gray so rapidly that the eye could hardly follow what was happening. In an instant the unusual animal had vanished, and in its place was a blazing column of fire. The great hall glowed with pulsating light, and a blistering, searing heat filled the room. The fireplaces sprang to life again and the chandeliers blazed with light. The horror that I felt at the appearance of the enormous horse was nothing compared to what I was now experiencing.

"The blazing column of fire vanished in a puff of smoke, leaving in its place a huge, ugly bird of prey. The creature was at least twenty feet tall. I slipped quietly behind a table, ready to dive beneath it if the bird decided to attack. The bird opened its tremendous beak, screeched three times, and then changed into an enormous bullock."

The minstrel shook his head. "It is almost too much to describe, my lord. The creature before us kept transforming itself rapidly, changing from one form to another so swiftly that we could hardly follow it. Gigantic rabbits, snakes, doves, harts, horses—we saw them all within a moment's time. At last, the creature took the form of an old man." The minstrel paused. "The old man was... was you, my lord."

Josiah glanced at Sir Faithful, but the elderly steward sat quietly. His face showed no emotion. "Minstrel, you say that you saw me at the Castle of Compromise?"

"Aye, my lord. I had seen you in the Village of Dedication, so when the creature took your form, I recognized you easily."

"Morphina the enchantress," Sir Faithful said quietly. "She was vaunting herself."

Wanderer's face registered his surprise. "Aye, my lord, it was Morphina indeed. You amaze me, sire. As we watched, the old man slowly changed into a wrinkled old hag with stringy hair and a dirty gown. 'I have come,' she cried, 'to show you my latest triumph over King Emmanuel.' With these words, she produced an enormous apple from the folds of her gown. The apple was nearly the size of a pumpkin, my lord. She held it overhead with both hands, crowing in delight as she did. 'This was in the possession of His Majesty, King Emmanuel, but within a fortnight I shall deliver it to His Highness, Lord Argamor. The entire kingdom of Terrestria shall then be his.'"

Wanderer cleared his throat. "As we watched, sire, the enormous apple split open to reveal a small crown of solid crystal, with a base of pure gold."

"The Crown of Kuros was carved from a single diamond," Sir Faithful interjected. "It was diamond that you saw, not crystal."

The minstrel nodded to show that he stood corrected. "Morphina held the crown overhead. The look on her face told us that she considered the theft of the crown quite an accomplishment. 'The Crown of Kuros,' she cried, dancing about with glee. 'Once it is in the hands of Lord Argamor, the entire kingdom of Terrestria will be his! Together, we shall wrest the kingdom from Emmanuel!' "

"Morphina is wrong," Sir Faithful said sternly. "The kingdom will never fall to Argamor. His Majesty, King Emmanuel, reigns supreme—and always shall. But we must not allow the Crown of Kuros to reach Argamor's hands."

"Aye, my lord." The minstrel bowed, and then continued. "After she had paraded around the great hall with the crown for another moment or two, she closed the apple around it," Wanderer reported. "Changing herself into a huge red dragon, she rushed from the castle, taking the apple with her." The minstrel sighed. "I came as fast as I could, my lord. I thought that you should know what had happened to the Crown of Kuros."

Sir Faithful smiled. "We are grateful."

The steward turned to one of the servants. "Allow Wanderer to spend the night in the great hall with the others. His service to the castle will not go unrewarded."

Sir Watchful stepped forward at that moment. He and Sir Faithful stood talking in quiet tones for several minutes while the rest of the court waited patiently. Josiah knew that they were discussing the theft of the Crown of Kuros, the revelation that it was indeed in the hands of Morphina, and what to do about it. At last, the castle steward and the castle constable turned and faced the crowd.

"Residents of the Castle of Faith, you are loyal servants to His Majesty, King Emmanuel," Sir Faithful declared in a voice that carried across the great hall. "You have heard the news that Wanderer has brought. The Crown of Kuros is indeed in the wicked hands of Morphina. The crown must be returned to the Castle of Faith. It must not fall into the hands of Argamor!"

He paused, and the court waited expectantly. "Tomorrow, Sir Watchful and I shall ride forth on a quest to locate and re-cover the crown for His Majesty. We shall enlist volunteers to help in the search. I would ask that any able-bodied man who loves his King and is willing to join in the quest step forward at this time."

Prince Josiah was the first to rise to his feet and step forward.

The next morning at daybreak, heavy chains rattled in the gatehouse as the castle drawbridge was lowered. The castle gates swung open and then chains rattled again as the portcul-lis was raised. A cavalcade of well-armed knights rode forward across the drawbridge. They reined their restless chargers to a halt at the far side of the moat. Sir Faithful, mounted on a handsome gray charger, wheeled his horse and then stood in the stirrups and addressed the knights.

"We shall ride in small groups," he instructed the men. "We are looking for the enchantress Morphina. When we find her, we will find the Crown of Kuros. As many of you know,

Morphina is very vain, and cannot resist showing off her powers wherever she goes. She should not be hard to locate."

The steward's gaze swept across the faces of the eager knights, and he seemed pleased. "Last night most of you heard Wanderer's report. Morphina is in possession of the crown, and for some reason, has not yet surrendered it to Argamor. We must find her and recover the crown before she delivers it to Argamor. Should Argamor gain possession of the Crown of Kuros, the results would be harmful for His Majesty's kingdom. Remember, men, we ride in King Emmanuel's name, and to uphold his honor. Throw your very heart and soul into this quest for your King. You have your assignments. Let's ride!"

Moments later small groups of knights rode in various directions from the Castle of Faith. Prince Josiah and Prince Selwyn had been assigned to ride with Sir Faithful and Sir Dedication. The latter was a small, wiry man with graying hair and a huge Adam's apple that constantly bobbed up and down in his scrawny neck. He rode a small, tired-looking horse that looked as it might drop in its tracks at any moment. Josiah had seen Sir Dedication around the Castle of Faith from time to time, but he had never had direct contact with the man.

The sun peeked from behind a cloud as the two young princes rode along behind Sir Faithful and Sir Dedication. Josiah reined his horse, a big bay mare, in close to Selwyn's mount, which was a sleek, black stallion. "Did you ever see a knight as skinny as Sir Dedication?" Josiah whispered. "He doesn't look strong enough to wield a sword in battle, does he?"

Selwyn shrugged. "He may be stronger than he appears at first glance. He has a reputation as a stalwart, courageous knight."

Josiah just smiled and refrained from giving voice to the thought that crossed his mind just then.

Following a narrow roadway, the four riders entered a quiet valley. A small stream meandered along the edge of the road and then crossed beneath a stone bridge. Dense forests bordered the valley on both sides. "The road forks just ahead," Sir Faithful told the others. "Prince Josiah, you and Prince Selwyn take the lane to the left. Within ten or twelve furlongs your road will meet up with ours again."

Moments later, just as the steward had said, the riders came to a place where the road forked. Selwyn and Josiah followed the road to the left. Within a furlong or two they came to a small clearing. The ringing sound of an axe echoed across the stillness of the morning. A tall, sturdy woodsman was felling a tall oak. He paused, lowered his axe, and wiped his brow as the two princes rode by.

"Good morning, my lords!" the woodsman called. "Pleasant day, is it not?"

"Aye, that it is, sire," Josiah replied, reining to a stop and standing in the stirrups. "We are on a quest for King Emmanuel, sire, and could use your help. The wicked enchantress, Morphina, has stolen the Crown of Kuros from the Castle of Faith. We must find her before she gives it to Argamor. Have you seen anything unusual, sire, that would tell you that Morphina had passed this way?"

The woodsman laughed as he approached the horses. "Is it that important to find Morphina, my lords?"

Josiah was puzzled by the man's unconcern. "The crown must not fall into Argamor's hands, sire! All of Terrestria will suffer the consequences if it does."

The woodsman shrugged. "I would hardly say that, my lord."

"But, sire, do you not realize the significance of the Crown of Kuros? Imagine what would happen if Argamor were lord of Terrestria!"

"Perhaps it would not be as bad as you imagine, my lord. I know that King Emmanuel has ruled Terrestria for eons, but perhaps it is time for a change. Personally, I could swear allegiance to either one."

Josiah could not believe what he was hearing. Here was one of King Emmanuel's subjects, a man who enjoyed the privileges of living in Terrestria under His Majesty's gentle reign, declaring that he would just as soon be ruled by Argamor! The young prince shuddered. How could anyone say such things? If only this man could see Argamor for what he really was—an evil, cruel, and treacherous tyrant who enjoyed seeing others suffer at his hands!

Selwyn spoke. "Have you seen any sign of Morphina, sire?"

"Nay, my lords," the woodsman replied. He turned and walked back to the task of chopping down the tree. The two princes rode on.

Josiah shook his head. "Can you imagine anyone saying that he would just as soon be ruled by Argamor?" He spurred his horse forward.

His thoughts turned to the quest for the Crown of Kuros. *If Selwyn and I could find Morphina and recover the crown,* he told himself, *we'd be heroes at the castle! All the lords and ladies would treat us with the utmost respect. Perhaps we would become the most important people in the castle. Our names would become known throughout all Terrestria. We would be famous. Prince Josiah and Prince Selwyn— the mighty warriors who saved the kingdom for King Emmanuel!*

He smiled inwardly. *And just think what would happen if I could find the crown by myself. That would be even better. Imagine! My name would be known far and wide. Prince Josiah—the knight who saved Terrestria!*

For the moment, the young prince forgot the urgency of recovering the Crown of Kuros and simply enjoyed the visions of grandeur. Selfish ambition and pride overcame his desire to serve his King. His motives for attempting to recover the crown were not to honor and glorify Emmanuel; he began to desire the glory for himself.

Selwyn rode close to Josiah. "What are you thinking about?"

Josiah looked up in surprise. "Uh, I was just thinking about the Crown of Kuros," he replied.

The two young princes rode carefully through the valley, stopping at each cottage or farm or huntsman's shack to inquire discreetly about Morphina and the Crown of Kuros. They learned nothing. The humble people of the district had seen and heard nothing amiss. By early afternoon, Josiah and Selwyn were tired and hungry.

The road dipped down into a ravine and crossed a tiny stream, then climbed a gentle rise and met up with the other road. Josiah and Selwyn rode up out of the ravine to find Sir Faithful and Sir Dedication standing under a tree talking while their horses grazed nearby. The boys reined in ten paces away. Josiah's heart leaped. Behind Sir Faithful and Sir Dedication, hidden in the shadows and unseen by either man, stood a knight in full armor, silently watching their every move.

Chapter Five

Prince Josiah spurred his horse forward. "Sir Faithful!" The steward looked up, and Josiah pointed at the strange knight.

Sir Faithful looked, and then glanced quickly at Sir Dedication. Placing his hand on the hilt of his sword, he strode across the clearing toward the knight. As he approached the mysterious warrior, he called out, "Welcome, stranger! Come join our quest for King Emmanuel, if you are pleased to do so."

The knight did not respond; the only movement was the flutter of a narrow blue streamer fastened to the knight's lance. Sir Faithful paused a moment, and then, when there was still no response, said, "Are you for us or against us?" Again, the knight did not respond; he remained as motionless as the tree beneath which he stood. "Is there something that you desire, sire?" the steward asked determinedly.

The knight moved. He lowered his lance and pointed it at Sir Faithful's chest. Josiah caught his breath. Sir Faithful's hand tightened on the handle of his sword, but he did not draw it. "Are you challenging me to fight?" he asked.

The mysterious knight did not move. His lance was still pointed at Sir Faithful's chest.

"Sire, would you at least let me know what it is that you desire from us? I have no idea what you are after, nor have my companions. Are you challenging us to a fight?"

The knight nodded.

"Well," the steward grunted, "at last we're getting somewhere. Would you at least tell us why you want to fight a complete stranger?"

The knight shook his head.

"If we refuse to fight you, will you leave us alone?"

Again, the knight shook his head.

"All right, then," Sir Faithful said, and Josiah could tell that he was irritated by the delay, "I'll fight you."

The silent knight shook his head. Turning his back on Sir Faithful, he strode rapidly across the road and pointed his lance at Josiah. "M-me, s-sire?" the young prince stammered. "Y-you want to fight m-me?"

The mysterious knight nodded. Beckoning with a gauntleted hand, he strode into the trees and mounted a big warhorse tethered in the shadows. He turned in the saddle and sat motionless, as if waiting for Josiah to follow.

"Sire, what should I do?" the young prince called to Sir Faithful, not at all sure that he should accept the unknown warrior's challenge.

"Accept his challenge in the name of King Emmanuel," the steward replied. "We will accompany you. We might as well see this thing through to the end." Josiah shuddered as he imagined what that end might be.

The mysterious knight led King Emmanuel's four knights

down a winding path that moments later opened into a huge meadow. Josiah was surprised to see nearly three dozen mounted knights waiting at the end of the meadow. As the questing party rode out of the woods, one lone knight rode forward a few paces. Reining to a halt in front of his companions, he raised his lance and waited. "He's challenging us to a joust," Sir Faithful said quietly.

The mysterious knight pointed at Prince Josiah and then pointed to the far end of the meadow, to a point opposite the challenger. The young prince gulped nervously, not at all sure that he should accept the challenge. But the mysterious knight had already dismounted and received a lance from a young squire who had run forward, and he was now thrusting it into Josiah's trembling hands with an insistence that told the boy he was not about to take "no" for an answer. Josiah looked to Sir Faithful for help.

"Accept his challenge," the steward said quietly. "Defeat him in the name of your King!"

Josiah nodded nervously. Gripping the lance with all his strength, he turned the mare and rode to a position opposite the challenger. He raised the lance. The challenger raised his lance in salute, and then before Josiah had fully realized what was happening, he and the challenger were galloping toward each other. They came together with a resounding crash that echoed across the hillside. The young prince felt the force of the impact through the shaft of his lance, and then, to his amazement, was dimly aware that the challenger appeared to be flying backward off his horse. He landed on his back to the accompaniment of clattering armor.

Josiah was amazed as he quieted the mare with a pat on the neck. *I won!* he congratulated himself, half in pride, half in astonishment. *I actually beat that knight!*

As he turned the mare, a group of beautiful girls surrounded the horse, laughing and giggling and calling Josiah's name. "Josiah the magnificent!" they chanted. "Josiah the magnificent! Ride again, Prince Josiah!"

Ladies, wait until you see this next pass, Josiah thought grandly. *You have not yet seen my best!*

Determined to impress the girls, Josiah rode the mare to his original position at the end of the meadow. A second knight rode forward, raised his lance in salute, and then spurred his horse forward. Josiah put the spurs to his own horse, leaned forward in the saddle, and steadied his lance against the jolting of the horse. A moment later his lance exploded into a thousand splinters and he felt a jarring impact against his armor that lifted him from his saddle, flinging him upwards and backwards. He landed on his back with a bone-jarring crash that knocked the wind out of him.

Josiah raised himself, dazedly shook his head, and looked about for his horse. The noisy group of girls were gathered around the victorious knight, cheering wildly and calling his name. Josiah snorted in disgust. "How embarrassing," he muttered, "to take such a fall in front of all those girls. One minute I'm the champion; the next, I'm lying on my back in the dust!"

Picking himself up from the ground, he limped painfully back to the mare. Disdaining to remount, he simply led her back to the tree where Sir Faithful and Sir Dedication waited. Ashamed to meet the steward's gaze, the young prince dropped his head and looked at the ground.

Prince Selwyn rode next against the challengers. He managed to unseat the first two knights, but was defeated by the third.

The mysterious knight rode forward and pointed his lance at Sir Dedication, indicating that the slender knight was to ride next. Sir Dedication mounted his aging horse and accepted the lance that was placed in his hands by a young squire. Josiah watched him ride to the end of the meadow. *What chance does Sir Dedication have?* he thought resignedly. *The other knights outweigh him, and he hardly seems strong enough to hold a lance. And his horse—it will be a miracle if that nag can get up to a full gallop! This is not going to be good.*

He turned and looked toward the group of knights to see who would be Sir Dedication's challenger. His heart sank. The knight riding into position was a huge, broad-shouldered warrior astride a powerful black stallion! The big warhorse snorted and pawed the ground. Sir Dedication and his feeble horse didn't stand a chance.

Sir Dedication and the challenging knight were now in position. They raised their lances in salute and then galloped across the meadow toward each other. Josiah knew what was about to happen, but he still felt himself compelled to watch. The powerful black thundered across the meadow. The rhythm of his hooves rang out like a death knell for Sir Dedication. Josiah winced as the two knights met at full gallop.

The groan of dismay died in his throat. To his utter astonishment, the brawny challenger tumbled backwards from his saddle! The powerful black warhorse staggered once, twice, and then went to his knees in the grass! He struggled to his feet, wheeled about, and then ran riderless across the meadow, confused and disoriented. Another knight galloped forward and caught his reins.

While Josiah stared in amazement, Sir Dedication rode into position for another jousting pass. Two lances were raised in salute; two horses galloped toward each other. Moments later, Sir Dedication had successfully unseated another opponent.

A ruby sun was dropping behind the pine-shrouded hills to the west as Sir Faithful sat beside an open fire, broiling fish taken from the placid lake beside which they were camped. Sir Dedication and Prince Selwyn were down by the lake, polishing armor. Prince Josiah walked over to the campfire and dropped to a seat on a fallen log. "That smells good, sire," he told the old man. "I'm hungry!"

Sir Faithful smiled. "There's nothing quite like fresh-caught fish grilled over an open fire," he agreed. "Dinner will be served shortly, Josiah."

Josiah picked up a stick and stirred the coals. "About the jousting today," he ventured.

Sir Faithful looked up from the fire. "Aye?"

"How did..." Josiah paused, uncertain how to phrase the question. "Sire, Sir Dedication is...is so frail-looking, and his horse looks...well, it looks like it's ready to fall over! How did... how did he manage to defeat all of the challengers? He went against thirty different knights, sire, and defeated every one of them. I don't understand it."

The old steward rotated the branch on which the fish were cooking. "Sir Dedication's strength comes from his heart, Josiah."

The young prince was puzzled. "His heart, sire?"

"His heart is fully dedicated to the service of His Majesty, King Emmanuel. Sir Dedication lives and breathes to serve his King. His greatest desire in life is to bring honor and glory to King Emmanuel. His tremendous strength in battle is the result of his pure heart, a heart wholly yielded and dedicated to the will of his King."

The steward pulled the skewer of fish from the fire and examined it closely, then returned it to the fire. "At present, we are on a quest for the Crown of Kuros. The crown must be recovered for His Majesty; it must not be allowed to fall into the treacherous hands of Argamor. As you know, Argamor and his evil forces are becoming bolder every day. His attacks on the people of Terrestria are becoming more and more frequent. He is determined to wrest the kingdom from Emmanuel."

Josiah thought it over. "Is there... is there the slightest chance that—that Argamor could somehow take the kingdom?" he asked hesitantly. "His Majesty is so wise and so powerful, but what if all of Terrestria sided with Argamor? Might Argamor then take the kingdom?"

Sir Faithful laughed quietly. "The kingdom is secure, my prince. Argamor is a mere grasshopper fighting a lion."

Prince Josiah sat back, reassured.

"The real battle is in the hearts of men and women, my prince. It behooves us to yield our hearts fully to the will of His Majesty, in order that there be no place for Argamor. Sir Dedication was victorious in the jousting today because his heart is fully yielded to his King."

The young prince had just one more question. "Whose men were those today? Why did they challenge us?"

Sir Faithful shrugged. "I think you know the answer, my prince. If not, ponder it for awhile."

The moon was full that night, hanging low in the sky like a huge silver coin displayed against black velvet. The rippling waters of the lake whispered gently to Josiah as he and his companions lay quietly beside the dying fire. The young prince thought about the jousting that afternoon, and about what the elderly steward had told him afterward. Sir Dedication, frail as he looked, had conquered each and every challenger because his heart was pure and wholly dedicated to his King.

Josiah sighed. His own heart was full of love and gratitude for King Emmanuel—he could never forget the day that his wondrous King had set him free—but deep down, he knew that his heart was not fully surrendered, as Sir Dedication's was. His own heart was rebellious at times, and selfish, and—why, oh why, couldn't his heart be yielded fully to the will of King Emmanuel, as Sir Dedication's was?

He sighed again and rolled over on his side.

He thought once again about the Crown of Kuros. How could the evil Morphina have opened the door to the keep and stolen the crown? Sir Faithful and Sir Watchful were so careful to keep the treasure vault securely locked. Sir Faithful must have been right when he surmised that the enchantress had gained access to the crown through the help of someone within the castle. He shivered as he wondered who that person could be.

An owl hooted from a nearby tree. Josiah rose up from his pallet and glanced around the campsite. Selwyn and the two men were already asleep. The embers of the campfire were pulsating orange and yellow and blue in their death struggles.

He glanced toward the lake, noting with delight that the moon had created a shimmering, silvery path across the surface of the water. "The Lake of Destiny," Sir Faithful had called it, explaining that legend claimed that a man could explore his own future by visiting the lake. A loon called from across the lake and Josiah shivered. The loon's call was so lonely... so mournful. He sat and stared out at the shimmering water. What did his future hold? If only it were true that the lake could tell him!

He heard the tiniest whisper of a sound and turned from the lake, starting in fright as he saw a wispy figure shrouded in white. He blinked, rubbed his eyes sleepily, and looked again. The figure was gone now, but he was certain he had seen her—a tall, slender woman dressed in a flowing white gown, standing silently just beyond the dying fire. He sighed. "Aye, it's been a long day," he whispered. "Time to get to sleep."

He stared again. The tall, slender white figure, so gossamer and transparent that he could still see the rocks and trees behind her, again had silently appeared just beyond the fire. As he watched, awestruck, the apparition became translucent, and then solid. The lady had a pleasant, friendly face, framed softly by long, golden hair. Her pearl-white gown fluttered gently in the breeze. In her left hand she held a single rose, a deep crimson blossom that glowed with a light all its own, and with her right hand she was slowly plucking the petals and dropping them to the ground.

"Prince Josiah," she whispered softly, and her voice was the gentle sound of a summer breeze, "I have come to show you the future. Your future. If your heart is open, my prince, what you see tonight will change you forever."

She moved closer, still dropping crimson rose petals.

Josiah sat rigid, uncertain as to what to say or do. He felt no fear; he somehow sensed that the ethereal visitor was kind and beneficent. At last, he rose slowly to his feet. "What am I to do, my lady?"

"Two paths lie ahead of you, my prince. You must choose wisely. If you would see what lies ahead, walk into the lake."

"Walk *into* the lake, my lady?"

"Aye," she replied quietly. "The Lake of Destiny can show you what lies ahead for you, in order that you might choose the path that you would take. Prince Josiah, if your heart cries out for surrender to your King, take this brief journey. Look ahead in order that you may choose your path wisely."

The woman moved silently toward the water. Josiah found himself compelled to follow.

She paused at the water's edge, standing at the very point where the shimmering path began. "Follow the silver path, Prince Josiah. You need not fear the water; the lake itself will take you into the realm of what lies ahead in order that you might learn and profit."

Josiah stepped to the water's edge. He hesitated for the tiniest moment and then stepped into the shimmering silver path on the moonlit waters. At once he felt two overwhelming sensations—the thrill of eager anticipation and at the same time, a deep and settled peace.

Chapter Six

Prince Josiah's heart was pounding furiously as he waded out into the rippling waters of the Lake of Destiny. The water swirled around his knees, but there was no sensation of cold wetness as he had expected. He waded deeper. When the water reached his waist, he paused in a moment of uncertainty, but the white lady called to him reassuringly. "Do not fear, Prince Josiah. You are about to view the future as it could be. If your heart is open, my prince, this night will change your life forever."

Josiah stepped forward. The water grew deeper. He felt a moment of panic when the waters closed about his shoulders, but he pushed resolutely forward. Still he felt no sensation of cold water around his body, and he wondered about it. It seemed that the waters of the lake had no substance, as if they weren't really there. *Perhaps this is an enchanted lake,* he thought, strangely detached and unconcerned as he walked deeper.

He looked up to notice a shimmering, silvery ceiling just above his head and briefly wondered what it could be. The answer hit him like a blow from a broadsword. He was looking *up* at the *surface* of the lake! He was submerged beneath the water! He was awestruck to realize that he had already passed beneath the surface of the lake, and yet, still he could breathe.

Josiah saw a sudden flash of light. For just an instant, he felt dizzy and nauseous, and he closed his eyes. He opened them to discover that his surroundings had changed. Shading his eyes against the sudden brightness that surrounded him, he looked around. He was standing in the middle of a narrow lane in broad daylight. Judging from the position of the sun, he estimated that it was late afternoon. He glanced upward. Somehow, the shimmering ceiling had disappeared and he realized that he was no longer beneath the waters of the lake. He had stepped through a doorway into another world.

Just ahead, partially hidden in a tangle of weeds and brambles, stood the ruins of a large castle. Rotting timbers leaned against crumbling walls and towers. Fallen blocks of white stone littered the ground. A slight depression in the earth showed where the moat had once been, but it had long ago been filled in with earth and debris. Crumbling fragments of wood were all that remained of the once-sturdy drawbridge. Curious, the young prince ventured closer.

As he stepped closer to the decaying wall and approached the opening that had once been the main gate, a raucous screech from just above his head caused him to jump with fright. He looked up. Three huge ravens sat atop the ruined wall, opening and closing their beaks as they watched him with beady eyes. "This castle, once so elegant and proud," he said aloud just to hear the sound of his own voice, "is now the home of dirty scavenger birds." He decided against going into the ruins.

Josiah heard a slight noise and turned just in time to catch a glimpse of a red fox darting through a hole in the wall. Intrigued, he decided to follow it. Ducking through the breach in the wall, he pushed through a tangle of briars and entered the castle ruins. He found himself in the barbican, the narrow courtyard between the outer and inner walls of the castle. The barbican was choked with weeds. Beneath a gnarled and twisted eucalyptus tree, he saw the crumbled remains of a once elegant stone bench. Passing through a breach in the inner wall, he entered the bailey, or castle courtyard.

Josiah paused and surveyed the ruined courtyard. Before him lay a scene of neglect and decay. An enormous fountain, once beautiful but now shattered and broken, occupied a place of prominence. Leading from the fountain was a narrow stone channel, now cluttered with boulders and debris. Piles of marble and mortar lay scattered about. The young prince felt a pang of remorse as he studied the now silent ruins. "This castle, once so beautiful," he sighed aloud, "now the habitation of ravens and foxes. Such a shame! I wonder what happened."

Strange, unexplainable sensations swept over the young prince. Recognition. Shadowed memories. An indescribable sense of loss, as though a friend had just died. *This castle is laid out much like the Castle of Faith,* he realized. *It's so very similar, and I almost feel that I have been here before. I wonder when it was built, and how long it has been abandoned.*

As Josiah stepped carefully over a pile of debris, the sunlight glinted on a half-buried object, catching his attention. He stooped and tried to pull the object free, but it wouldn't move. After kicking some of the dirt away with the pointed toe of his saboton, he was finally able to pull it free. He stared. He was holding a badly dented war shield.

Laying the shield face down in the grass and weeds, he rubbed it vigorously back and forth to scrub off some of the dirt caked on the face. He gasped when he turned the shield back over. The coat of arms on the shield was that of King Emmanuel.

"Get out!" an angry voice called. "Get out of here!" Josiah looked up in alarm to see an old man hobbling furiously toward him. "Get out of my castle, you dirty, worthless cur!" The man wore a blue-and-black doublet with long sleeves, a sleeveless jerkin of pale deerskin, and a magnificent cloak of blue and gold. His clothing, now faded and worn and threadbare, had at one time been elegant. His regal garments proclaimed that he had once seen better times.

"My apologies, my lord," Josiah stammered, taking a step backwards. "When I saw that the castle was in ruins, I assumed that no one lived here."

"Get out! Get out, I say! This castle is my home, not yours!" the old man replied sharply, as if offended by Josiah's words. "Do you think that I am going to feed every mangy stray that wanders in?"

"Sire, I am not a mangy stray," Josiah said hotly. "I am Prince Josiah, son and heir to His Majesty, King Emmanuel." He watched the old man closely. The hermit—for that's what Josiah had already decided the old man was—carried a long, crooked staff in his gnarled hands, and the young prince half expected the man to use it on him. His angry face was lined with years of cares and worries. His lips were curled with an expression of bitterness, and his dark eyes mirrored his hatred of life and everything about it. Josiah decided that he had never before seen anyone so cross and spiteful.

"Get out!" the hermit snapped crossly. "I'll not have the likes of you in my castle!" To Josiah's astonishment, the old man dropped his staff, bent over, and picked up several large stones. Drawing his hand back, he advanced menacingly. "I'll teach you to enter my castle without being bidden!"

"I-I didn't know that there was anyone here," Josiah explained again. "I saw a fox come in through a hole in the wall, and I simply followed it."

The old man grasped a rock in his right hand and tensed his arm as if preparing to hurl it. "I gave you a chance to get out," he snarled. "You dirty animal! Now you'll wish that you had."

What can I say? Josiah thought desperately. *I've already tried to explain myself!*

The hermit moved toward the young prince and raised his arm to hurl the rock at him. As he did, his cloak fell open. Josiah gasped. The man's deerskin jerkin bore the King's coat of arms! *Who is this hermit?* the boy wondered. *At one time he must have served King Emmanuel, for he wears His Majesty's coat of arms. But why is he so irritable and bitter?*

"Off with you, dirty varmint!" the hermit shouted. "Off with you, before I strike you with a rock and then give you a good drubbing with my stave!"

Josiah backed away. "I'm leaving, sire. I'm sorry for intruding."

The cross old hermit suddenly hurled the rock straight at Josiah. The young prince saw it coming but could not get out of the way in time. The missile struck him squarely in the chest. Feeling no pain, he looked down in astonishment. The rock had passed right through him! His mind raced. *How can this be possible?*

He heard a yelp, and spun around. A half-grown yellow puppy, long-legged and flop-eared and clumsy, tucked his tail between his legs and scrambled to get out of the way of another flying rock. The hermit's anger was directed at the dog, not at Josiah!

He hurled another rock, and then another and another. "Get out!" he screamed in fury. "Get out of my castle!" The puppy scrambled for the hole in the wall.

"Sire, he's just a puppy," Josiah called, coming to the defense of the stray dog. "He's not going to hurt anything. He probably just wandered in looking for food or something."

The man seized his staff and rushed forward, swinging it with all his might. Josiah leaped to one side to avoid being clobbered. But just as before, the angry hermit was after the dog, not the young prince. Red-faced with rage, he swung wildly at the stray puppy, but the terrified animal had already decided that he had stayed long enough. He fled through a hole in the wall.

Grumbling to himself, the man turned and climbed a flight of crumbling stairs. "Today I am taking a trip that I have long dreaded, and this worthless, mangy mutt has to make an appearance."

Just then Josiah realized that the cranky old hermit could neither see nor hear him. "I'm a visitor from another dimension in time," he said aloud, "so why should I be surprised that he acts as if I am not here?" The old man, of course, did not hear him.

The hermit began carrying huge bundles down to an ancient oxcart waiting inside the remains of the castle gatehouse. After countless trips down the crumbling stairs and across the cluttered courtyard, the oxcart was so heavily loaded that it could not possibly hold any more. "What is all this stuff?" Josiah felt compelled to ask, watching as the man hefted the last bundle on top of the load. "It looks to me to be just scraps of wood and straw. Is it worth anything?"

The old man said nothing. He began carefully lashing the

load in place. "Have to hitch up those stubborn oxen," he grumbled to himself. "Then I leave this miserable place for good."

As Josiah followed the old man across the courtyard, he
again got the uneasy feeling that he had seen the castle before.
The structure was in shambles, and yet, somehow it seemed so
familiar. The hermit entered the stables and soon returned with
a pair of lumbering oxen which he hitched up to the heavily
loaded cart. "Get along now!" he shouted, slashing at the oxen
with a stout willow switch. "We've a good ways to go before
sundown." He drove the oxen through the opening in the wall,
across the shallow depression that had once been the moat,
and out onto the road. Josiah fell in step beside him. It seemed
the natural thing to do. He glanced skyward. Less than an hour
until sunset, he figured, and yet the old hermit was just setting
forth on a journey.

"Where will your journey take you, sire?" he ventured to ask.

The old hermit walked along in stony silence, and the young
prince remembered that the strange old man could neither see
nor hear him. But after a long moment or two, his strange companion began to speak in a quiet, sad voice. "Today I must go to
stand before my King," he said slowly. His voice faltered. "I-I
am not ready. Woe is me."

Josiah was awestruck. "King Emmanuel?" he whispered. "You
will see King Emmanuel?"

The hermit shook his head sadly. "If only I—" He dropped
his head and fell silent.

The journey was not a pleasant one. The old hermit grumbled and complained and muttered to himself as the oxen
lumbered along. The road they followed headed due west and

the old man complained repeatedly that the sun hurt his eyes. When one of the huge wooden wheels on the oxcart began to squeak, he complained bitterly about the noise. More than once he grumbled about the fact that the stray puppy had trespassed within his castle, and Josiah wondered why such a small thing should cause the old man to become so agitated.

How can anyone be so grouchy and cross? the young prince asked himself. *I hope that I do not become like this when I am old.* Watching the hermit, he finally came to the conclusion that the miserable old man was afraid. *If he is indeed to stand before King Emmanuel today, why is he not filled with joy, instead of fear? A meeting with His Majesty should be a wondrous occasion!*

The sun was a fiery red ball low on the horizon when at last they came to a broad, slow-moving river. The old man brought the oxen to a stop at the water's edge and stood gazing across to the opposite bank. His eyes seemed to be filled with sorrow and regret, and Josiah's heart was moved with sympathy. For a moment, the young prince studied the flowing water and wondered how they would ever cross.

Josiah glanced across toward the far shore and his heart leaped like a quail exploding from a thicket. Situated just beyond the river was a glistening city whose walls appeared to be built of solid gold. The city seemed to gleam with a light that rivaled that of the sun. He was seeing the Golden City! It was the most majestic, most beautiful sight that he had ever seen. "Is that—is that the City of the Redeemed?" His heart was filled with wonder.

"The Golden City," the hermit said quietly, as if he had heard Josiah's question. He stared across the broad river. "Aye, if only I had come prepared." His voice was filled with anxiety and regret. Josiah wondered why he seemed distressed at the sight of the beautiful city instead of being overjoyed. He glanced at the old man and saw to his surprise that he was weeping. With a trembling hand, the hermit led the oxen forward. He gave a deep sigh of resignation and stepped into the water.

Josiah sensed that he could not make the crossing with the old man, so he stayed where he was and simply watched. When the oxcart reached deeper water, it began to float. Soon the oxen were swimming. The old man pushed ahead resolutely. The water never reached his shoulders. Josiah was surprised at how easily he made the crossing.

As the old man stepped from the water on the opposite shore, a regal figure moved from the gate of the city and hurried to meet him. Josiah's heart leaped. King Emmanuel! The gracious King greeted the old hermit warmly. "Welcome home, my son! Welcome to the Golden City of the Redeemed. We have anxiously awaited your arrival."

The hermit fell to his knees at King Emmanuel's feet. "My Lord!"

"The Golden City is your eternal home," the monarch said quietly. "Welcome home."

The hermit rose to his feet. He gestured toward the heavily loaded cart where the two oxen waited patiently. "Here is what I have to present, Your Majesty." He lowered his head.

Although the far shore of the river was more than two furlongs away, Josiah could clearly see and hear the scene as if he were standing a few paces away.

"We will see if it passes the test," King Emmanuel said. At a gesture from his hand, two bright beings in shimmering robes hurried forward with flaming torches. As Josiah watched in disbelief, they unhitched the oxen, led them away a short distance and then set fire to the oxcart and its contents. Soon the flames were leaping so high that Josiah could see their flickering reflections on the golden walls of the city.

As the fire burned down, Josiah was amazed to see that there was nothing left of the oxcart and its load but a small, smoldering pile of ashes. The old hermit stared in dismay at the smoking heap. King Emmanuel stepped toward him. "Have you nothing to present to me, my son? Each day of your life was an opportunity to lay up treasures for the Golden City, but you have brought nothing but wood, hay, and stubble. Have you nothing to offer me?"

"Nay, my Lord." The old man bowed his head, tears coursing down his cheeks, as he stood empty-handed before his King. "I have nothing to offer."

Josiah turned away. His heart went out to the old hermit, cross and complaining though he was, as he thought about the unhappy scene that he had just witnessed. What a disappointment, what a heartbreak, to finally reach the Golden City of the Redeemed and stand before King Emmanuel with nothing to offer! The sun dropped behind the hills just then, plunging the riverbank into abrupt darkness. Josiah turned back toward the Golden City and saw that it was still ablaze with light.

Still pondering the heartbreaking scene that he had just witnessed, the young prince retraced his steps. Moments later, as he followed the road up a gentle slope, he looked up to see the shimmering silver surface just above his head. As he climbed higher, he abruptly broke through the surface and found himself emerging from the Lake of Destiny. The moon was now high overhead.

He stepped from the lake and walked across the sandy lakeshore, surprised to find that his clothing was not even wet. A white form moved in the darkness ahead. The ethereal lady was waiting for him.

"Josiah, my prince," she greeted him. "How went the journey?"

"It was disheartening, my lady." Briefly, he told her about meeting the old hermit in the ruins of the castle, accompanying him to the river crossing, and witnessing the meeting with King Emmanuel. "He had nothing to offer King Emmanuel," he told her soberly. "When the fire had finished burning, there was nothing left but a tiny pile of ashes." He sighed. "The old hermit was grouchy and cross and selfish, but I still felt sorry for him when he stood empty-handed before the King. It was as if his entire life had been reduced to nothing."

"Prince Josiah, do you know why he had nothing to present to His Majesty?"

Josiah shook his head. "Nay, my lady, I do not know."

"His life, like the castle you saw, was empty and wasted, for his heart was not yielded to his King. He lived for himself, my prince. In this life, he did serve King Emmanuel, but his motivation was selfish vainglory, not the honor and glory of his King. As a result, the trial by fire reduced his life's accomplishments to ashes."

Josiah sadly shook his head. "I do not want to finish as he did. One day I want to stand before my King and know that he was pleased with me, that I have brought him honor and glory."

He paused as a thought occurred suddenly. "I did not even learn the hermit's name."

The white lady looked at him strangely. "You know him, my prince. Did you not recognize him?"

Josiah frowned. "Nay, my lady, I did not know him. I had never seen him before."

She stepped closer. Her left hand still clutched the stem of the rose, but the petals were gone. "You have just visited the future, Prince Josiah. You have seen destiny as it may unfold, but the meeting with King Emmanuel does not have to be as you saw it. You have the power to change that future meeting. The selfish old hermit that you saw, my prince, was you."

Chapter Seven

Prince Josiah was stunned by the words of the white lady. He stared at her for several moments, utterly speechless. Finally, he found his voice. "Me?" he cried. "The hermit was me? How could that old man be me?"

"You have seen the future, or what the future may hold for you, my prince, if your heart is not surrendered wholly to the will of King Emmanuel. One day you will go to the Golden City of the Redeemed—there is no doubt of that since you are a child of the King—but you may go empty-handed. Do you want to stand before His Majesty in that fashion?"

Josiah wept at the woman's words. "Nay, my lady! I do not want my life journey to end like that. I eagerly await my trip to the Golden City, but I do not want to go if I have nothing to offer King Emmanuel. What can I do to change the outcome? I want my life to honor and glorify my King, and I do not want to stand before him empty-handed. What can I do?"

The lady looked at him kindly. "You must surrender your will to the will of King Emmanuel, Prince Josiah. Your heart must be yielded totally to him. Then you will bring honor to his name, and then you can expect to stand before him one day and hear him say, 'Well done.' "

"But I am serving him," Josiah protested. "Right now I am on a quest for him to try to recover the Crown of Kuros."

"Aye, but your heart is not fully yielded," she said softly. "Remember yesterday, when you wanted to watch the archery tournament instead of completing your mission for King Emmanuel? Sir Faithful summoned you three times before you finally took him the parchments, and then your heart was filled with impatience and resentment because you were missing the tournament. Prince Josiah, can you honestly say that your heart is yielded to your King?"

Josiah hung his head. "How do you know these things, my lady?"

"You have already met my elder brother, Sir Wisdom," she replied. Josiah looked up in surprise, and she gave him a gentle smile. "My name is Lady Prudence. I was sent to help you make the decision to yield your heart fully to your King."

"I know that my heart is not fully yielded to King Emmanuel, my lady, and I so want it to be, but... but it is so hard! It is as if there are two parts to me—one part would yield completely while the other part wants to be selfish and unyielded! It is as if I hear two voices inside, one bidding me to do good and the other bidding me to do evil."

The lady nodded. "Aye, my prince, you are closer to the truth of it than you realize. You do have two natures, and they do battle constantly." She moved closer and put a gentle hand on his arm. "I want you to visit the future one more time. I want you to see the results of a life that is yielded to His Majesty.

The man that you will visit is the man that you could become if you surrender your heart wholly to your King. Walk into the lake again, Prince Josiah, for there is more that you must see. If your heart is open, what you observe this time will change you forever." With those words, she was gone.

Josiah was deep in thought as he turned toward the Lake of Destiny. He walked fearlessly into the waters and waded out quickly until they closed over his head. Looking up, he again saw the shimmering silvery surface above him. Moments later, he found himself walking across a sunny meadow bright with wildflowers. Butterflies danced in the air to the accompaniment of cheerful melodies sung by the many songbirds in the tree-tops. The atmosphere in the meadow was one of vibrant life.

Prince Josiah walked across the meadow and climbed a small rise. He saw a castle of white marble rising above the trees of the forest and so he hurried toward it. Soon he came to a well-traveled road that led through the forest to the castle. The young prince whistled a cheerful tune as he followed the road. He rounded a bend and saw a humble daub-and-wattle cottage beside the road. Standing at the door of the cottage was a nobleman dressed in elegant clothing. He was holding the lead rope of a healthy looking brown-and-white cow.

"Nay, my lord," came a woman's voice from inside the cottage. "Please take the cow away, sire." Knowing that the nobleman and the woman could not see him, Josiah hurried closer. He saw a young peasant woman with flaming red hair and a pleasant, friendly face. Two young children, a boy and a girl, clutched the skirts of her homespun dress. The children had hair the color of polished copper.

"The cow is for you, my good woman," the nobleman told her. "These little ones of yours could use the milk—is that not so?"

The woman eyed the cow longingly. "I cannot accept the cow, though one can see at a glance that she is a fine animal and would be a good milker. My husband has been sick, my lord, and we have no money."

The nobleman smiled. He knelt at the woman's feet and reached out a gentle hand toward the little girl, who shyly put her tiny hand in his. The man winked at the little girl and then stood to his feet. "Apparently I have not made myself clear, my good woman. The cow is a gift. I want nothing in return. My stableman tells me that this is my best milker, and I want you to have her. She'll provide you with plenty of good, rich milk for these two fine children of yours. You can make butter and curds and cheese. The cow is simply a gift, good woman."

The woman glanced at the cow again and then shook her head. "Nay, we cannot take the cow, my lord. We have no way to pay you back. As I said, my husband has been sick for weeks."

The nobleman nodded. "Aye, I'm sorry about your husband, my good woman, and I wish him a speedy return to health. But please do not rob me of a blessing by refusing to take the cow. She is a gift to you and your family. I want nothing in return; you do not have to worry about paying me back."

The peasant woman looked at the cow again and burst into tears. "Why are you doing this, my lord? What have we done to deserve such kindness?"

"I am simply trying to help a neighbor in need. Your family is facing a difficult time right now, and this is one way that

I can be of assistance. I am simply following the orders of His Majesty, King Emmanuel. His book tells us that it is more glorious to give to others than to receive from others."

He held the lead rope toward the weeping woman. "Here— please accept this small gift at my hand. My King would have me do this for you, good woman. Please do not deny me the opportunity to obey him."

The woman reached out a trembling hand and took the rope. "I thank you, my lord. You will never know what this means to us. We shall never forget you."

The nobleman smiled. Reaching within his doublet, he withdrew a small, leather bag and handed it toward her. "This will also help until your husband is able to work again."

She drew back. "Nay, my lord! We can never accept that! You have already done so much for us by giving us this magnificent milk cow."

"His Majesty would have me do this for you," the man said quietly. "As a servant to King Emmanuel, I must wholly follow his will. Would you deny me the opportunity of obeying him, or the chance to honor his name by helping you?"

The woman let out a deep sigh as she reached for the money. "Bless you, kind sire, bless you! We shall never forget your kindness." She smiled suddenly. "It is no wonder that the people of this region love you so well, my lord. You have the heart of a king!"

The nobleman smiled. "I am grateful for the opportunity to serve my King in this way. With your permission, my good woman, I will secure the cow in your shed and then make my way back to my castle. I am expecting a messenger from the

Golden City of the Redeemed at any moment." Taking the lead
rope from the woman, he turned away from the door. As he
turned, Josiah saw an old man with a kind face and lively eyes
that radiated warmth and friendliness. Here was a nobleman
who was happy and radiant in the service of his King.

Moments later the cow was contentedly munching hay from
the manger in the shed. The elderly nobleman hurried toward
the road. "My Prince," the peasant woman called from the cottage door, "we are grateful for your kindness, my lord! We shall
never forget what you have done for us!"

The elderly nobleman smiled and waved. Josiah fell in step
beside him, fully aware that the old man could not see him. Less
than a hundred paces from the cottage, the aging prince threw
back his head, opened his mouth, and sang a song of praise to
King Emmanuel.

Josiah and the old man were nearing the magnificent white
castle when a servant approached with a parchment in his hand.
"A message for you, my lord, from His Majesty. It came from
the Golden City just now." He handed the document to the aging prince.

The old man broke the King's seal on the document, unrolled
it, and scanned it eagerly. As he read, his eyes lit up with pleasure and anticipation. The servant noticed. "Good news, my
lord?"

"The best news of all, Gawain!" the old man replied happily. "This is the news for which I have been waiting. King
Emmanuel has summoned me to the Golden City of the
Redeemed. I am to stand before him this very day!" He
clutched his wrinkled hands together in a gesture of eagerness,
and his face was radiant. "Just think, Gawain, I shall see King

Emmanuel face to face before this very day is out! What a wondrous meeting this shall be!"

He re-rolled the parchment and handed it back to the servant. "We must hurry back to the castle, Gawain. I shall prepare to leave for the Golden City at once."

Twenty minutes later—or at least it seemed to Josiah that it had been about twenty minutes, though he was not certain that time was measured in the same way here—the old man was ready to begin his journey. The inhabitants of the castle had gathered around the heavily loaded oxcart, and the courtyard had rung with their tearful but joyous good-byes. As the old man had bid farewell to each and every person, Josiah had sensed the deep love and caring that the nobleman had for each, and yet, he could tell that the old man was impatient to start for the Golden City.

At last, the farewells were said and the oxen were lumbering along a road that was familiar to Josiah. The old man's eyes sparkled with eager anticipation as he walked along. Never before had Josiah seen anyone so happy. The aging prince radiated enthusiasm. There was a spring in his step and an expression of wonderment on his face. He threw back his head and broke into a familiar song of praise.

> "I sing the greatness of my King, my Lord Emmanuel
> His power is great and far exceeds
> What mortal tongue or pen can tell.
> My heart is full; I sing for him,
> And trust that I may serve him well."

Tears filled Josiah's eyes as he listened to the song of gratitude that poured from the lips of the happy old man. Here was a man who loved King Emmanuel with all of his heart, and it was obvious to Josiah that his heart was yielded fully to the will of his King. His life was one of joy and victory. The young prince found himself almost envious. If only his own heart could be yielded to King Emmanuel as this man's was!

When the old man came to the second stanza, Josiah joined in.

"I sing the love of my great King, my Lord Emmanuel.
His lovingkindness ransomed me,
But why he did, I cannot tell.
His love led him to die for me,
I trust that I may serve him well."

Josiah looked up to notice that the sun was sinking below the horizon. The western sky was a panorama of brilliant color as the old man and the oxcart reached the banks of the broad river that had to be crossed in order to reach the Golden City. When the old man caught a glimpse of the Golden City, he leaped high into the air and cried out for sheer joy. "My home! My eternal home! Soon I shall see the face of my beloved King, Emmanuel!" Tears of joy flowed down the man's wrinkled cheeks. Josiah stared at him in amazement. Never before had he seen anyone so overcome with sheer joy.

The old man eagerly led the oxen into the river. "Golden City of the Redeemed," he cried exuberantly, "open wide your gates to me, for I am coming home! Emmanuel, my King, I am eager to behold your face! My Lord, I am coming home!"

The water grew deeper, and before long, the oxen were swimming. The oxcart, loaded as it was, floated so low in the water that Josiah feared that it was in danger of sinking. The waters swirled around the old man's shoulders as he reached the middle of the river. In no time at all he walked from the waters to stand safely upon the distant shore. The oxen leaned into the yoke and struggled to pull the heavy cart up onto the bank. The crossing had taken but a moment.

King Emmanuel stepped from the gate of the Golden City. The old man ran to meet him, throwing himself down at the monarch's feet. "My blessed Master," he cried aloud. "It is only of your grace and mercy that I am here, my Lord."

King Emmanuel lifted him to his feet and embraced him. "Welcome home, my son. Welcome to the Golden City of the Redeemed. Your arrival is cause for celebration."

Tears of joy again flowed down the old man's face. "My Lord, my King! My heart is filled with such gratitude that my poor lips cannot express it. I shall never forget that blessed day when the Coach of Grace came to me and I saw your wondrous face for the first time!" Bowing his head, he again knelt at King Emmanuel's feet.

"My son, I have loved you with an everlasting love," the monarch said quietly. "The Golden City is your eternal abode. Welcome home."

Although the far shore of the river was more than two furlongs away, Josiah could clearly see and hear the scene as if he were standing just paces away. Watching the tender scene from across the river, Josiah suddenly felt an overwhelming desire to be in the presence of King Emmanuel. He longed to enter the Golden City and be forever with him. He moved toward the river. "Not yet, Prince Josiah," a voice within him seemed to say. "The time has not yet come for you to cross the river. You must wait until your King summons you to the Golden City."

Disappointed, the young prince came to a standstill at the water's edge. He continued to look longingly across the river.

The nobleman rose to his feet. He gestured toward the heavily loaded cart where the two oxen waited patiently. "Here is what I have to present, my Lord."

"That which you have to offer will be subjected to the trial by fire," King Emmanuel said. At a gesture from his hand, two bright beings in shimmering robes hurried forward with flaming torches. As Josiah watched, they unhitched the oxen, led them away a short distance and then set fire to the oxcart and its contents. Soon the flames were leaping so high that Josiah could see their flickering reflections on the golden walls of the city.

As the fire burned down, Josiah was amazed to see a huge pile of glittering treasure where the oxcart had stood just moments before. King Emmanuel stepped forward. "Gold, silver, and precious stones," he said, and Josiah could tell from his voice that he was pleased with the old nobleman. "Your life has honored me, my son. Well done! You have served me faithfully. Enter into the joy of your Lord."

Together, arm in arm, the King and the enraptured nobleman strolled into the Golden City. A number of bright beings in shimmering robes hurried forward and began to carry the glittering treasure into the city. Josiah stood on the riverbank and watched until King Emmanuel, the nobleman, and the bright beings had disappeared through the magnificent gate. With a sigh of longing that he could not explain he turned away and began his journey back to the present.

As Josiah emerged from the Lake of Destiny, he found the white lady waiting for him at the campsite. "Josiah, my prince," she greeted him, "how went the journey?"

Josiah suddenly found that he was so overwhelmed by what he had just witnessed that for a moment he could not even speak. The lady waited patiently as he struggled with his emotions. "I want," he finally managed to say, "I want my journey to the Golden City to be just like that! King Emmanuel was pleased with the treasure that the old man presented to him. He told the man that his life had honored him. I too want to please my King; I want my life to honor him. I want King Emmanuel to say 'Well done' when I stand before him."

Lady Prudence smiled gently. "Josiah, my prince, you know why the old man heard the words 'Well done' from the lips of his King, do you not? His heart is yielded to King Emmanuel, and therefore his life honored the King. His life's accomplishments withstood the trial by fire because they were achieved in the King's name, and for His Majesty's honor and glory. The treasure that you saw after the fire will last forever as a testimony to the grace of King Emmanuel."

"I want that," Josiah said quietly. "I want my life to honor my King."

"Then you must yield your heart to Emmanuel," the white lady replied gently. With those words she vanished, leaving Josiah to stare into the empty darkness of the night.

With a deep sigh of longing, the young prince made his way back to the campsite where Prince Selwyn, Sir Faithful, and Sir Dedication lay sleeping around the dying campfire. He dropped to his knees on his bedroll. His mind was in turmoil as he pondered the glimpses of the future that he had just seen.

"My journey to the Golden City must not end as that cross old hermit's did," he whispered to himself. "I must live my life so that I bring honor to the name of King Emmanuel! When I stand before him, I want to present him with treasures that will last forever. I want to hear him say, 'Well done; you have been a good servant.'" Josiah lay down, and was asleep in moments.

Chapter Eight

Prince Josiah awoke the next morning to the smell of fish frying. He sat up sleepily, rubbed his eyes, and looked around. The morning was young and the sun was just beginning to peek over the ridges to the east. A thick white fog hovered just above the ground. Josiah turned. The Lake of Destiny was invisible, lost from view in a swirling sea of white mist.

"Did you sleep well?" Sir Faithful's words startled the young prince, and he turned to see the castle steward busy over a crackling, snapping fire. "The fish will be done in less than five minutes, Josiah. We also have roasting ears and roasted potatoes." Josiah nodded drowsily.

His mind went back to the events of the night before. Had he really walked into the lake, or had he just been dreaming? Had he really seen the future? The visit to the ruins of the hermit's castle, the journey to the Golden City, the experiences with the joyous nobleman, the meeting with King Emmanuel—last night it had all seemed so real, but was it? *Perhaps I was just dreaming,* he told himself, but the very idea was a source of disappointment. *Perhaps I saw some sort of a vision. Perhaps I will never know if the visits to the Golden City were real or not, but this one thing I do know—I do not want to stand before my King empty-handed!*

He thought about the Crown of Kuros. *What if I could some-how recover the crown for King Emmanuel, and thereby bring honor to his name? Wouldn't it be grand if I could find the crown and bring it back to its proper place in the Castle of Faith? It would not matter if I received honor. In fact, it would not matter if no one else in the castle ever found out who brought it back.*

He set his jaw in determination. *I will do my best to find the Crown of Kuros and restore it to its proper place in the treasure vault of the Castle of Faith. But I will do it in secret, so that no one else will know. Then the honor and the glory will go to King Emmanuel.*

It was just two days ago that Morphina gained access to the keep and stole the crown, but already it seems like it has been a hundred years! In his imagination, Josiah found himself just outside the door to the vault as he remembered what had happened on that fateful day. "You may return to the archery tournament," Sir Faithful was saying. "But first, lock the door of the keep behind me."

"How do I do that?" Josiah asked.

"Just push the door shut and pull the handle down," Sir Faithful replied, moving toward the entrance to the vault. "The door will lock." He hurried away, leaving the young prince standing alone at the massive door.

Prince Josiah reached out and pushed against the iron door with one hand. The massive barrier refused to move. Setting the lamp on the floor, the young prince placed both hands high on the door and leaned against it with all his strength. With a creak of protesting hinges, the huge door began to move—slow-ly at first and then faster and faster until it clanged shut. Josiah reached for the handle.

Just then a distant noise reached the ears of the young prince.

He paused, listening intently, and his eyes widened in dismay. Even though he was deep within the heart of the Castle of Faith, he could hear the sounds of a wildly cheering crowd. His heart sank. The tournament! Something crucial had just taken place at the archery tournament, and he had missed it! Snatching the lamp from the floor, he hurried from the tunnel, handing the lamp to the guards as he passed.

Josiah caught his breath as he visualized the events of that fateful moment. He had closed the door of the vault—he remembered that distinctly—but had he locked it? Just at the moment that he was reaching for the handle, he had heard the noise of the crowd at the tournament. *Did I lock the door? I closed it, but did I lock it?*

Josiah closed his eyes as he struggled with the question. Concentrating as hard as he could, he tried to remember. He could still feel the cold steel of the massive door as his fingertips touched it, feel the tremendous weight as he pushed against it with all his strength, hear the squeak of the hinges and then the heavy clank as the door slammed shut. But had he locked it? He couldn't remember. The question haunted him.

"I just wanted to be sure that you are certain, Josiah. Morphina could not have gotten into the keep without help from someone within the castle." Sir Faithful's words in the great hall that night came back to torment him. *I'm not certain that I locked the door, not certain at all! What if I am the one who allowed that wicked Morphina to enter the King's treasure vault and steal the Crown of Kuros?* The thought brought anguish to his heart.

"Josiah! Are you ready to eat breakfast?" The young prince looked up, startled, and Sir Faithful laughed. "I've called you three times, Josiah. Whatever were you thinking about?"

Prince Selwyn and Sir Dedication laughed as Josiah stood to his feet with the hot blush of embarrassment creeping across his face and neck. His ears burned. "I was just—just... oh, never mind, sire."

The steward smiled gently. "Come have some breakfast, lad. We have a long day ahead of us."

Josiah walked toward the fire. A spot of bright color on the ground nearby caught his attention, and he glanced toward it. He caught his breath. Lying in the grass were three rose petals of deep crimson.

After breakfast the four riders mounted up and rode throughout the countryside, stopping at each cottage and farm they saw along the way. They questioned each person they came to, trying to pick up the trail of Morphina and the Crown of Kuros, but no one could offer them any helpful information. Some of the King's subjects expressed concern when they learned that the crown had been stolen; others were apathetic and indifferent when told of the loss. To Josiah's dismay, a few even seemed delighted at the idea of the crown falling into Argamor's hands.

It was early afternoon when they approached a bustling city nestled in the rugged foothills of a tall, pine-shrouded mountain. "We'll split up and go separate ways in order to talk to more people," Sir Faithful told the others, reining his horse to a stop just outside the gate of the city. "Josiah, you and Selwyn search the east end of town; Sir Dedication and I will search the west side. Keep your eyes open. You may even encounter some opposition, so be alert and be prepared. As you work your way through town, try to stay in sight of each other. We will meet at the north gate in three hours." The search party rode through the gate, and the two men turned their mounts to the west.

Selwyn and Josiah rode slowly down a narrow street. Tiny shops and cottages lined both sides of the lane. The city was bustling with activity, as busy as an anthill in the summertime. Peasants and merchants hurried here and there on various errands; vendors cried out as they competed with one another for the attention of prospective customers. "I still wonder who could have allowed the enchantress to open the King's treasure vault," Selwyn remarked aloud. "I just cannot imagine anyone within the Castle of Faith doing such a thing! Everyone at the castle seems so loyal to His Majesty."

Josiah said nothing.

"Well, doesn't it perplex you?" his companion persisted. "I just cannot figure it out."

"Why don't you take that side of the street," Josiah suggested, pointing, "while I take this side?" The boys dismounted, and, leading their horses, began to walk through the noisy throng of people.

"There's a livery stable," Selwyn pointed out. "We can leave our horses there while we go afoot." The boys left their mounts in the stable and began the search for Morphina and the Crown of Kuros.

"What does it matter, my lord?" a cobbler asked Josiah a few minutes later, looking up from his work over the pair of spectacles perched at the end of his nose. "Why is it so important to recover the crown for Emmanuel?"

"His Majesty is the rightful King of Terrestria," the young prince asserted. "The Crown of Kuros must not fall into the hands of Argamor!"

The cobbler shrugged. "I hear all this talk about the great King Emmanuel," he said with a sneer, "but I do not even know that he exists! I have never seen him. I have never heard his voice. And yet, everywhere I go, I am told that the King wants us to do this, or does not want us to do that. If you ask me, my lord, this King of yours has no right to rule my life! I did not choose him as King. I am not even sure that he exists. Why should a King whom I have never seen tell me what to do? I will rule my own life. For all I care, this precious crown of yours would be better placed in the hands of Lord Argamor!"

Josiah was shocked at the man's words. "King Emmanuel is the rightful Lord over Terrestria," he protested. "The kingdom belongs to him and him alone! He made this kingdom and everything in it."

The cobbler snorted. "Surely you do not expect me to believe that, my lord. Emmanuel did not make Terrestria; this kingdom made itself."

"Made itself?" Josiah echoed. "Sire, that is preposterous! How could this land make itself?"

The man laughed derisively. "Some of the greatest scholars in the kingdom have proved it with their studies, my lord. Terrestria did make itself and everything within it. King Emmanuel is a tyrant who rules us from a distant city, but I want no part of his kingdom. Now, if you will excuse me, I must return to my work." He disappeared into the back of his shop.

Josiah was dismayed at the cobbler's words. How could

anyone in Terrestria not love and praise and follow King Emmanuel? How could anyone claim that the kingdom had made itself, and that His Majesty had no right to rule? How could anyone refuse to recognize Emmanuel's authority and therefore not yield his heart to the will of the King?

An hour later, as Josiah was leaving the shop of a lamp merchant, he spotted Sir Faithful hurrying toward him. "How has your search progressed so far, my prince?" the old steward asked, stroking his beard with one hand.

Josiah shook his head. "We have learned nothing yet, sire."

Sir Faithful looked up and down the narrow, crowded street. "Where is Prince Selwyn?"

"I think he's across the street in the harness shop," Josiah answered. "Do you want me to summon him?"

"Nay, let him alone," the steward said quickly. "But I need you to come with me and give me some assistance." Josiah obligingly fell in step with the old man.

"We have questioned many people today, sire," Josiah told Sir Faithful, "but no one seems to know anything of Morphina or the Crown of Kuros. You told us that if the enchantress were here, she would be easy to find. If no one here seems to know of her, should we not leave and search elsewhere?"

Sir Faithful nodded agreeably. "Perhaps that would be wise." He shot a sly look in Josiah's direction. "You realize, of course, that Morphina is far more clever than you can imagine. She can deceive the best minds in the kingdom! If indeed she is the one who has stolen the Crown of Kuros, it will not be an easy matter to get it back. Anyone who attempts it might possibly forfeit his life. Are you certain that you are willing to pay so high a price?"

Josiah looked at him in surprise. "Sire, you sound as if you are trying to talk me out of trying to recover the crown for King Emmanuel."

The old man shrugged. "I'm not trying to talk you out of it—I'm simply telling you that this quest might turn out to be quite dangerous. I want you to be certain that you are willing to risk your life in this quest. If not, you may want to reconsider before you go any further."

"Are you saying that I should turn back and return to the Castle of Faith?"

"Not necessarily, Josiah. I'm just saying that you need to be aware of the risks involved. It's the same way with this matter of yielding your heart to King Emmanuel—it is a good thing to do, and yet, there are some huge costs that you should take into consideration. You may not be quite ready to take such a step; at least not until you know everything that is involved."

Josiah frowned. He had never heard Sir Faithful talk this way, and he found it confusing. "Sire, what are you saying? Do you think I am not ready to yield my heart fully to my King?"

"I'm saying that you should take it slowly. Such a decision is not to be taken lightly, and you do not want to jump into it. Think it through. As King Emmanuel himself has told us, it is better not to make a vow than to make one and then break it. Such a commitment may cost you more than you are ready to pay. My counsel is to take it slowly."

Josiah was silent as he pondered Sir Faithful's advice.

"The quest for the Crown of Kuros will possibly be far more difficult than we had anticipated," the old man said quietly. "Morphina is a formidable adversary, and we should not take her lightly. We need to decide if we are ready to suffer the losses that Morphina could inflict if we go against her."

The young prince shook his head in bewilderment. "But, sire, you told us that it would be a simple matter to find Morphina—that she was quite vain and cannot resist showing off her powers wherever she goes."

For some reason that Josiah could not comprehend, his words seemed to offend Sir Faithful. "I said nothing of the sort," the steward retorted, in a huff. "Mind your tongue, lad."

They walked in silence. To Josiah's surprise, Sir Faithful led him through the city gates and out into the craggy foothills at the base of the mountain. The terrain was rugged, with jagged outcroppings of red sandstone that pointed at the sky like giant fingers. Clusters of pine trees adorned the mountainside at irregular intervals. Josiah struggled to keep up as the old steward climbed a steep slope. "Sire, what are we doing out here?"

Sir Faithful turned to him with a look of delight on his wrinkled features. "I did not want to tell you while we were within the city, but I have found the Crown of Kuros! I knew that you would want to be the one to retrieve it, and so I came for you. It is in a place from which it will be rather difficult to recover it, but I have no doubt that you can do it. We will say nothing about the fact that I was the one who found it, and so, when we bring it back in triumph to the castle, the glory and honor will be yours. Tell me, Prince Josiah, are you ready for this venture?"

Josiah grinned. "Aye, sire. I am ready, sire. Lead me to it!"

Sir Faithful led him under the edge of an overhang of rock and into a deep grotto. A torch on the rocky wall illuminated a small cavern. "Be careful, my prince," the old man cautioned.

"Watch your step." Josiah saw a huge black hole in the floor of the cavern. Kneeling carefully at the brink, the young prince peered down into the darkness of a vertical shaft that seemed to disappear into the very heart of the earth.

"How deep is this pit?" Josiah asked, and his voice echoed and re-echoed up from the depths below.

"I suppose that there is no way to know unless one cared to jump in," the old man said with a laugh. He took the torch from the wall of the cavern and held it out over the pit. "Do you see that glimmer of light down on the ledge at the side? That is the Crown of Kuros, reflecting the light from the torch. Morphina has hidden it here."

Josiah was in awe. "That's the crown?" He lay on his belly, intently studying the glittering object far below. The Crown of Kuros—if indeed that was what it was—was at least forty or fifty feet below the rim of the rocky pit. Retrieving it would be a dangerous task. The young prince raised himself to his knees and looked at Sir Faithful. "Sire, if you knew that the crown was here, why were you telling me what a formidable adversary Morphina is, and how difficult it would be to get the crown from her? She is not even here!"

The old man grinned. "I was testing you, lad. I wanted to see just how determined you were to recover the crown."

"What is this place?" Josiah asked, gazing around at the cavern. "Why did Morphina hide the crown here?"

Sir Faithful hesitated. "This is the Cavern of Vainglory," he said at last.

The young prince glanced at the glimmer of light far below. "If that is the Crown of Kuros, how can we get it back?"

"Simply climb down and get it," his companion replied. "I will hold the torch for you."

Josiah drew back in fear. "Climb down the wall? Sir Faithful, this pit must be at least a hundred feet deep! Perhaps it is even deeper than that. One slip and I would fall to my death."

"Aye, this is a place of danger, but you can do it," the old man assured him. "You are young and strong. You are very agile, and very intelligent. You seem to perform well under pressure, and you always seem to be able to think your way out of difficult circumstances. I have no doubt that you can handle this. Would I send you into a perilous situation that you could not handle?"

Josiah hesitated. His heart pounded with fear. "I don't know that I can handle this one, sire."

"Have confidence in yourself," the old man urged. "You can do it! And think of the honor that will be yours when we come riding into the castle with the Crown of Kuros. You'll be the hero of the kingdom!"

The young prince took a deep breath. "All right, sire. Please hold the torch for me." Kneeling at the very brink of the chasm, he turned and lowered one trembling foot over the edge. His groping boot found a foothold on a small ledge and he rested his weight on it. Gripping the edge with both hands, he lowered his other foot.

The trip down into the darkness of the pit was perhaps the most frightening thing that Josiah had ever done. Moving slowly and carefully, making sure of each handhold or foothold before he trusted his weight to it, he crept down the slippery rock wall a few inches at a time. Ten or twelve feet below the rim of the pit, he paused to rest. Holding his breath, he ventured to look down. All he could see below him was a black, empty chasm engulfed in total darkness. "This is the scariest thing I've ever done in my life!" he called up to Sir Faithful. "In my life! In my life! In my life!" His voice echoed around him, a crescendo of sound that seemed to come back at him from all directions.

His companion chuckled. "You're doing just fine, Josiah. Just tell yourself, 'I can do it; I can do it!' And think of the way that people will treat you when we come back to the castle with the crown. You'll be a hero!"

Josiah shifted his weight to his left foot and reached down with his right, groping with his toes for a foothold. At that moment, the spur of rock broke away beneath his left foot and he found himself falling into the darkness below. "Sir Faithful!" His scream of terror echoed throughout the cavern.

Chapter Nine

Prince Josiah fell through the darkness, flailing his arms and clutching frantically at the emptiness of the void around him. Emptiness. Darkness. Nothing but thin air. There was nothing to grab onto, nothing to arrest his fall. His heart constricted in terror as he plummeted into the emptiness and darkness of the pit.

Splash! Instead of striking a rocky bottom as he had expected, he landed in a deep pool of water. Gasping for breath, he lunged upward. When his head finally broke the surface, he inhaled gratefully. Treading water frantically with his hands, he took a second breath and looked upward. The flickering torch was gone; above him was nothing but inky blackness. Sir Faithful had left him!

"Sir Faithful!" he screamed, "I'm alive! Help me!" The echoes of his own voice crescendoed around him in the darkness, mocking and tormenting him. "Sir Faithful! Help me! There's deep water down here, so I didn't get hurt, but I'm in danger of drowning. Help me!"

There was no answer. The darkness above him was silent.

Struggling to keep his head above water, Josiah swam straight in one direction until he bumped into a wall of stone. He clawed at it, trying desperately to find a handhold, but the surface was smooth and unbroken, affording him no grip of any kind. He stared about in the darkness, but still could see absolutely nothing. His face dipped beneath the water and he lunged upward, coughing and sputtering. He was desperate. The weight of his armor was pulling him under and it was all he could do to keep from sinking. His strength was ebbing quickly.

The book! His book would provide him with light! Reaching into his doublet, he snatched the volume and flung it open. The pages began to glow with a soft, white light and he could now see that he was in a roughly circular chamber about thirty feet across. His heart leaped. To his right, just a few feet away, was a crevice in the rock wall just above the waterline. It was small, but it would be enough to allow him a handhold. He lunged toward it, thrusting the fingers of his free hand into the crack and pulling himself upward so that his face was free of the water. Gratefully he rested, panting like a winded horse while he caught his breath.

He studied the cavern around him. Just beyond him was a rough opening in the wall, and the water about him was gently flowing into it. The ceiling of the cavern was less than two feet above the water at that point. "So I fell into an underground river," he said aloud. He turned the book toward the opening and the pages glowed brighter and brighter. "This is the way out," he said, encouraged and hopeful.

Still clinging to the rock, he tilted his head back. "Sir Faithful!" he shouted. "Can you hear me?"

The only answer he received was the echoes of his own voice. *Why would Sir Faithful desert me like this?* he wondered. *He's one of the best friends I have—why would he leave me at the one time that I needed him the most?*

Releasing his hold in the crevice, Josiah swam toward the opening in the wall. When he reached it, he discovered to his delight that his sabotons touched bottom. He could stand! Holding his book above the water, Josiah followed the course of the subterranean river. The water was just deep enough to reach to his chin, though in some places it was deeper and he was forced to swim short distances. The pages of his book glowed brighter and brighter, reassuring him that he was indeed following the passage that would lead him out of the cavern.

After half an hour of swimming and wading the course of the underground stream, the exhausted young prince saw a bright spot of white light in the darkness ahead. His heart leaped. Daylight! He pushed ahead, encouraged and rejuvenated by the sight. The circle of light grew larger and larger. The subterranean passage abruptly widened into a large cavern with huge, crystalline stalactites hanging from the ceiling. The stream widened at that point and became so shallow that it barely reached Josiah's knees. A sandy bank dotted with large outcroppings of sandstone led up a gentle slope to the bright blotch of daylight, an opening so large that a man could walk through it. Leaving the stream, Josiah scrambled up the slope and burst out into the sunshine.

Thoroughly spent from his ordeal in the cavern, the young prince dropped to a seat on a boulder and rested. He looked about in astonishment. He had emerged from the side of the mountain less than two hundred paces from the gates of the city! Resting his hands on his knees, he sat quietly for a few moments as he caught his breath.

Why did Sir Faithful desert me? he asked himself again. *Why would he run away and leave me at a time when I needed him so desperately? Why would he send me down into that treacherous pit without at least providing me with a rope?*

He thought about the tiny glimmer of light he had seen when he looked down into the pit. *How does Sir Faithful know that it was really the Crown of Kuros? All we could see was a tiny sparkle of light, but he was so sure that it was the crown! How could he possibly tell?* He frowned. *And how would he have found it there if he were searching in the city?* He shook his head and stood to his feet. Things just didn't make sense.

Hurrying back into the city, the young prince retraced his steps to the shop where Sir Faithful had found him. He searched the street, peering into shops and dodging peasants and merchants as he scanned the crowds for the sight of Selwyn. At last he found him at the city well, drinking thirstily from a gourd dipper while a goatherd waited.

Selwyn's eyes widened as he looked up from the vessel and saw him. "Josiah, where have you been? Sir Faithful was looking for you."

Josiah nodded to show that he already knew. "He found me."

Selwyn frowned as he handed the gourd back to the goatherd. "He was just here looking for you, Josiah. He left with Sir Dedication less than two minutes ago! They were called away on another quest for King Emmanuel—something to do with the Crown of Kuros, I believe. You and I are supposed to go back to the Castle of Faith." He looked at the goatherd. "I thank you, sire."

The two boys made their way down the busy street. "Sir

Faithful found me here about an hour ago," Josiah insisted. "He took me up to a cave on the side of the mountain, for he had found the Crown of Kuros and wanted me to help him recover it from a deep pit." Briefly, he told of falling into the darkened pit and of his ordeal in the underground stream. "And when I needed him the most, Sir Faithful deserted me! He just ran away without assisting me."

A look of disbelief spread slowly across Selwyn's face. "That's impossible, Josiah! Sir Faithful would never, never do that—and besides, he was just here looking for you. He said that he hadn't seen you since he and Sir Dedication left us at the gate."

"Well, he must have forgotten, then, because he was the one who took me up to the cavern."

"It couldn't have been him. Josiah, he was just here looking for you!"

An uneasy feeling swept over Josiah. "Then if it wasn't Sir Faithful who took me up to the cavern, who was it? It looked like him. It sounded like him. Selwyn, if it wasn't Sir Faithful—"

"Morphina!" both boys guessed at the same instant.

Selwyn groaned. "Josiah, you saw Morphina and didn't even know it."

Josiah shook his head in disbelief. "Selwyn, I was so sure it was Sir Faithful. It looked and sounded just like him. How could I have known—" Suddenly he was angry. "She tried to kill me by talking me into going down into that pit! I trusted her, thinking that it was Sir Faithful. And she tried to talk me out of continuing with the quest for the crown, and also out of surrendering my heart—" He stopped abruptly, but his friend didn't seem to notice.

"But couldn't you tell that it wasn't Sir Faithful?"

"I never even thought about it, Selwyn. She looked and sounded just like him! She was pretty convincing." Josiah looked thoughtfully at his companion. "What do we do now?"

Selwyn shrugged. "We've questioned just about everyone on this side of the city, so I suppose we just head back to the castle and wait for Sir Faithful."

The boys made their way to the stables, claimed their horses, and mounted up for the ride back to the Castle of Faith. Selwyn studied the sky as they rode through the city gates. "Looks like a storm coming," he observed. "We had better ride fast."

Josiah glanced skyward. Dark thunderclouds were rolling in ominously from the north, and a brisk wind was blowing in gusts, causing the trees to sway in unison like a troupe of dancers. "Aye," he agreed, "you are right. Let's ride!"

Fifteen minutes later, the two young riders descended a heather-carpeted slope and started across a wide plain between two rugged mountain ranges. A brilliant bolt of white-hot lightning slashed across the blackness of the heavens, lighting up the gloomy afternoon with an intense flash of white light. The wind suddenly howled in fury like a demented giant. A booming report of thunder crashed down around them, echoing back and forth between two mountain ranges. Huge drops of stinging rain occasionally pelted their faces.

"This is it!" Josiah shouted above the voice of the wind. "We're in for quite a storm!"

"Aye, that we are," Selwyn replied. His eyes suddenly grew wide and he stood in the stirrups. "Look!"

Josiah turned. Sweeping across the plain toward them with

the speed of a runaway horse was a solid curtain of pouring rain. It was as if the clouds were being sliced open by a giant knife. The downpour would be upon them within seconds, and they would be drenched immediately.

"There!" Selwyn shouted, turning in the stirrups and pointing to a huge projection of rock jutting out from the side of the mountain. He put the spurs to his mount and the horse leaped forward, racing for the safety of the sheltering overhang. Josiah was right behind him. They rode into the shelter of the huge ledge just ahead of the sweeping torrent of rain.

Both boys reined to a halt and dismounted. "That was close!" Josiah remarked as the boys walked their horses. "If we had been three seconds later, we would have gotten soaked. You saw this shelter just in time." A bolt of lightning flashed across the face of the storm, to be followed seconds later by an ear-splitting crash of thunder that seemed to shake the mountain.

Selwyn looked upward at the enormous rocky ledge above them as they led their mounts to the base of the mountain and tied the reins to the rocks. "Look at this place!" he said, with a note of awe in his voice. "Doesn't it almost look like the entrance to a castle or something?"

"It would be a mighty big castle," Josiah retorted. "The entire Castle of Faith would fit beneath this overhang, I believe. This ledge must be three hundred paces long!" He looked up. "How high would you say that is—seventy feet?"

A brilliant, prolonged flash of lightning followed by a stunning crash of thunder drowned out Selwyn's reply. The rain fell in torrents. A wall of water cascaded down from the end of the overhang less than fifteen paces from where the boys stood and then splashed out across the plain.

The sound of horses' hooves rang out above the violence of the storm, and both boys turned to see a dark knight ride at full gallop beneath the enormous overhang. The powerful warhorse snorted and pawed the flinty ground when his rider reined him to a stop. The knight dismounted and led his mount to the backside of the ledge. "One of Argamor's men!" Selwyn whispered.

Josiah's heart beat faster.

As the boys watched in silence, the dark knight reached up with a gauntleted fist and knocked six times on the rocky wall above him. The sound of steel striking rock echoed across the shelter. The knight paused, and then knocked six more times. After a second or two, he knocked again, striking the rock with his gauntlet exactly six more times. To the utter astonishment of the two young princes, the side of the mountain opened as if it were a giant door. The dark knight quickly mounted and rode forward, disappearing within the mountain. Seconds later, the opening had vanished.

"Did you see that?" Selwyn exclaimed, his eyes wide with astonishment. "It *is* an entrance! An entrance to an underground castle, perhaps!"

"Three sixes," Josiah replied. "He knocked on the mountain in three sets of sixes."

Josiah ran forward and examined the side of the mountain where the dark knight had entered, but it appeared to be a solid wall of rock. Without stopping to think about what he was doing, the young prince reached up and pounded his fist on the rocky wall six times. He paused, and then knocked six more times.

"Josiah, don't!"

But the young prince was already reaching upward and knocking six more times. Just as it had for the dark knight, the side of the mountain slowly opened, and the boys could see an enormous tunnel glowing with a soft blue light. Josiah stepped forward, but Selwyn hesitated. "Josiah, we don't know where it leads!"

"Hurry!" Josiah urged, striding forward into the tunnel. "Hurry, Selwyn, before it closes again!" Selwyn grimaced, and then leaped forward to stand beside Josiah. With the soft whoosh of escaping air, the mountain closed behind them.

Chapter Ten

"Josiah, why did you do it?" Prince Selwyn cried softly. "We don't know where this tunnel leads!"

"You didn't have to come in," Prince Josiah retorted.

"I came so that you wouldn't be facing danger by yourself," Selwyn replied. "If you get killed in here, no one would ever know what happened to you!"

The boys stared at the underground passage before them. The craggy tunnel, thirty feet high and thirty feet wide, glowed with a soft blue luminescence. The far end of the tunnel, nearly a hundred paces in the distance, was considerably darker than the entrance. Every few seconds, a brighter pulse of light would pass down the rocky corridor like a wave of the ocean traveling toward the shore.

"I've never seen anything like it," Selwyn said quietly. "Where does the light come from?"

"The rocks themselves are glowing," Josiah replied, stepping toward the closest wall to examine it more closely. "Nay, I was wrong. There are patches of thick, spongy substance covering them. This is where the light comes from. Look—you can see dark places on the rocks where some of it is missing."

Selwyn reached out and touched the glowing material. "Do you know what it is, Josiah?" he exclaimed. "It's little mushrooms, thousands and thousands of tiny little glowing mushrooms, each smaller than the tip of my little finger. Look—they're packed together so tightly that they appear to be a continuous, bumpy material. But they're mushrooms, I tell you, tiny little mushrooms." He stepped back and surveyed the glowing tunnel. "There must be thousands of millions of them in here!"

Josiah reached out an exploratory hand and pinched the luminescent substance. "Aye, you are right. It *is* little mushrooms. Look how the bands of brighter light pass down the corridor in waves. How are the mushrooms doing that?"

Selwyn and Josiah walked slowly down the tunnel, which angled sharply downward into the heart of the earth. The entire tunnel glowed with a soft blue light, but the brighter pulses of blue light passed over their heads every few seconds. "Watch closely," Josiah whispered, realizing for the first time that they were in a place of danger. "If anyone comes we'll hide behind one of the larger boulders."

They reached the lower end of the tunnel safely and paused to survey the extraordinary scene before them. The tunnel opened out into a huge cavern that stretched before them as far as the eye could see. The cavern was dark, lit only by occasional tall, slender forms that glowed with the familiar soft blue light. "Giant mushrooms," Josiah said softly. "The cavern is lit by giant glowing mushrooms!"

"Whoever saw mushrooms five feet tall?" Selwyn scoffed.

"The ones in the Land of Unbelief were almost this big," Josiah replied with a shrug. "These must be the full-grown versions of the little ones in the tunnel." He looked up at the ceiling, which appeared to be nearly two hundred feet above their heads. "Look, you can see small patches of pale blue light up there. That must also be clusters of the little glowing mushrooms."

Scanning the area carefully for any sign of danger, the boys cautiously stepped from the glowing tunnel and entered the enormous cavern. "It's darker in here than it was in the tunnel," Selwyn observed, "so it will be easier to hide if someone comes."

Josiah nodded. "It will also be easier for someone to ambush us," he replied in a whisper, drawing his sword and turning about repeatedly as he surveyed the unusual surroundings. Evil was lurking nearby—he could sense it—and he was determined to be alert and ready for conflict. The overwhelming sense of evil pervaded the atmosphere and a mysterious uneasiness grew stronger by the minute.

The cavern floor sloped gently down and away below them, and as his eyes grew accustomed to the darkness, Josiah began to make out the forms of countless buildings stretching away as far as the eye could see. "It's an underground city!" he exclaimed softly. "Look, Selwyn. There are hundreds and hundreds of buildings, maybe even thousands. It's an entire city, built underground!"

"Aye, that it is," Selwyn agreed. "I've never before seen the likes of it."

A winding road led from the tunnel down the side of the slope, and, without discussing what they were planning to do, both princes found themselves hiking down it. The giant glowing mushrooms were placed every ten paces or so, so the trail was reasonably well lit. Josiah ducked under one of the unusual growths and looked up at the bottom of the mushroom cap, which was nearly five feet across. Hundreds of wafer-thin gills were arranged around the stem like the spokes of a wheel; up inside the cap glowed an intense blue light that hurt his eyes when he looked at it. He ducked away, rubbing his eyes.

The road smoothed out as the boys followed it into the subterranean city. It had now become a regular street, passing by houses and various other buildings. Josiah noticed that the street meandered back and forth, twisting and winding like the track of a serpent. When the street intersected with other streets, he noticed that the other lanes were every bit as crooked. "Where are all the people?" Selwyn whispered. "If this is a city, there must be people."

"I don't know," Josiah replied in a whisper. "Stay alert. This is a place of intense evil; I can feel it. Draw your sword and be ready." Selwyn complied.

The boys crept forward silently. Moments later, Selwyn put his hand on Josiah's arm. "Down below us in the center of the city," he whispered. "Do you see it? I keep seeing a flickering orange glow."

"I noticed it," Josiah answered, "but I thought at first that perhaps it was merely my imagination. Let's go down and see what it is, shall we?"

They turned and followed a narrow lane that twisted and wound its way down the slope toward the strange orange glow. Soon they found their way blocked by a ring of huge boulders seven and eight feet high. The flickering glow seemed to come from just beyond the ring of boulders. "Listen!" Josiah exclaimed. The distant sounds of a vast throng of people drifted across the darkness of the cavern.

"Give me a boost," Selwyn requested. "I want to see what's on the other side of these rocks."

Interlocking his fingers, Josiah leaned over so that his friend could step into his hands. When Selwyn did so, the young prince lifted him until he could see over the top of the nearest boulder. Selwyn peered over the top for a few seconds, and then ducked back down. Josiah lowered him to the ground. "What did you see?"

"You won't believe it!" Selwyn whispered, and his eyes were wide. "It's a great, circular amphitheater with stone benches, and there are thousands and thousands of warriors there! That's why we haven't seen anybody—apparently, they're all gathered here. There's a raised stone platform in the center of the amphitheater, and a fire pit in the middle of that. That's what's causing the flickering light. I also saw half a dozen thrones around the fire, and each one has an important-looking man sitting in it. Josiah, it appears that some sort of ceremony is about to start."

"Follow me," Josiah said eagerly. "There has to be a way past these rocks. I don't think it would be wise to go over the top." He and Selwyn crept along the edge of the boulder ring, searching for a crack or crevice between the boulders that would allow them access to the huge amphitheater below. But the boulders had been placed so that they formed a tight, impenetrable wall, each boulder fitting tightly against the next. "We'll never find a way in," Josiah lamented.

"Get down!" Selwyn whispered fiercely. He dropped to the

ground and scrambled under the edge of one of the boulders. Josiah saw no cause for alarm, but he quickly followed. Seconds later, two burly sentries in black armor strolled past their hiding place. Both men wore huge swords on their belts and carried wands that glowed with a soft blue-white light.

"That was close," Josiah whispered, when the guards had passed. "I'm glad that you saw them in time."

"I wouldn't have if they hadn't carried the light wands," his friend replied.

"What do you suppose the wands were made of? They glow with the same blue light that the mushrooms do."

Selwyn shrugged. "I suppose that they were cut from the mushrooms. The guards are gone, Josiah. Shall we continue?"

At last, when the boys were about to despair of finding a way in, they came to a place where a boulder had shifted, creating a narrow gap between it and its neighbor. "Here!" Selwyn whispered exultantly. "We can watch from here."

He knelt at the base of the boulder and peered through the opening. Josiah joined him. The boys found themselves at the upper edge of a huge, fan-shaped amphitheater, with stone benches spread in a vast semicircle around a raised stone platform. Thousands and thousands of warriors in dark armor sat waiting expectantly. Just as Selwyn had described, a huge fire blazed in the center of the platform, lighting up the darkness of the cavern with a flickering orange light. Six stern-faced figures arrayed in full battle dress sat in huge stone chairs just back of the blazing fire. An air of tense expectancy hung over the vast throng of warriors.

"Who are these warriors?" Selwyn whispered. "There are thousands of them! And some of them are women."

"Sh-h!" Josiah pointed. "Look."

At that moment, a tall nobleman in regal garments strode forcefully across the stage. "Lords and ladies of the realm of darkness," he cried, and his powerful voice echoed across the vast amphitheater, "give homage to your lord and master! I give you the sovereign of the realm of darkness, Lord of the kingdom of Terrestria, our commander, Lord—"

The roar of the crowd drowned out the rest of his words. A huge man had appeared before them on the stage, arrayed in majestic garments of black and crimson. An enormous golden sword with a jeweled hilt swung at his side. With powerful shoulders, brawny arms, and a thick, black beard that covered his swarthy features, the warlord's presence was impressive, if not frightening. The vast throng of warriors sprang to their feet, cheering and brandishing swords and spears and leaping about in frenzy as their leader walked to the center of the stage.

"That man is not Lord of Terrestria," Selwyn declared passionately. "King Emmanuel is!"

The underground city rang with the frenzied shouts of the vast throng of dark-armored warriors. Josiah noticed that the fire blazed higher at the appearance of the powerful warlord. The light from the flames glistened on the well-polished sword at his belt.

"My loyal subjects," the huge man boomed, and a hush instantly swept across the crowd. As one, they sheathed their swords and dropped into their seats, lifting their faces in awed silence toward the speaker.

Josiah turned to Selwyn. "That's Argamor!" he whispered in astonishment. "I'd know that voice anywhere!"

"Then this underground city is Lower Terrestria," Selwyn replied. "It is the headquarters of Argamor and his warlords. I have heard of it, though I had never thought that I would see it."

"Lords and ladies of the realm of darkness," Argamor continued, "Terrestria will soon be ours!" The crowd erupted in thunderous applause. They leaped to their feet and the vast amphitheater rang again with the noise of their shouts. Countless swords waved overhead; armor rattled. At a gesture from their leader, the warriors sank quietly to their seats.

"Together, we shall rule Terrestria," Argamor promised in a voice that resonated across the vast cavern. "Together, we shall seize the throne of Emmanuel and throw off the shackles of his tyrannical rule. Terrestria shall be ours!"

Again, the crowd leaped to their feet and the amphitheater echoed with the sound of their frenzied shouts. Argamor made a small gesture with his hand and they immediately fell silent, dropping into their seats. The bearded warlord had them completely in his power.

"Our forces have gone against the armies of Emmanuel on numerous occasions in our quest for the kingdom," Argamor continued, "and we have experienced setbacks. Not defeats, mind you, but setbacks. We have learned from these battles. As a result of these setbacks, we are wiser and stronger than ever before. We are more determined than ever that the kingdom of Terrestria shall belong to us."

He paused, strolling across the stage and looking out across the vast sea of faces before him. As he turned, Josiah saw that the back of his billowing black cape was embroidered with the symbol of a fierce red dragon. The crowd waited expectantly.

"We are not ready to win the kingdom by direct conflict with Emmanuel's armies," Argamor declared. "At present, his forces are superior to ours. The power of the universe is in his hand. If we elect to go against his armies in direct conflict, we shall be defeated."

A groan of dismay swept across the crowd. Josiah turned to Selwyn. "I wonder why he is telling them this."

Argamor raised his voice. "But, my loyal subjects, we shall prevail! Terrestria will be ours! We shall indeed seize Emmanuel's throne! We shall not prevail by force, for we have learned that that is not yet an option. We shall prevail by strategy.

"We shall not win the kingdom by storming Emmanuel's castles and attacking his armies. Rather, we shall wrest the kingdom from the hand of Emmanuel by stealing the hearts of the King's subjects. One man at a time, one woman at a time, one heart at a time, until the entire realm of Terrestria belongs to us! The battle will be quiet, inconspicuous. Many of Emmanuel's subjects will not realize what is happening.

"I repeat—we shall conquer Emmanuel's kingdom one heart at a time. Our strategy shall be to steal the heart of every man, woman, and child in Terrestria. When this is accomplished, we shall then be in a position to seize the kingdom by force!"

Argamor paused. The vast throng sat silent for a moment as they pondered the warlord's words. Abruptly they leaped to

their feet as one man, cheering and shouting and applauding.
Swords and spears rattled like metallic leaves before an invisible
wind. The floor of the cavern shook. The fire behind Argamor
raged higher and higher until the flames were leaping more than
thirty feet into the air. Josiah covered his ears in an attempt
to block out the cacophony of sound. Argamor gestured; the
throng fell silent.

"I have asked the Council of Six to prepare strategy for this
quiet battle that shall one day deliver the kingdom into my
hands. The six captains that you see before you are trusted warriors of evil. You know them; they are some of my most capable
warlords. They have assured me that this strategy of winning
one heart at a time cannot fail. I ask you to give them your
attention."

Argamor turned, raised his right hand, and called, "Captain
Pleasure, I call on you to begin this council of war. If you please,
Captain, present your plans and strategy to overthrow the king-
dom of Emmanuel."

Josiah turned to Selwyn. "Pay close attention to everything
that these warlords say. We need to try to remember everything
so that we can report it back to the castle. King Emmanuel's
armies need to know what happens at this council of war!"

Chapter Eleven

Captain Pleasure stepped forward to the enthusiastic cheers of the vast throng in the darkened amphitheater. The captain was a tall man with a handsome face and a winning smile. His coat of arms bore the images of a castle and a court jester. "My lord, Lord Argamor," he said, bowing to the bearded warlord, who had taken a position to one side of the stage, "I am honored to be in your service."

He turned to the eager crowd of dark-armored warriors. "Fellow servants of the rightful Lord of Terrestria, the great and powerful Lord Argamor, lend me your ears. Our worthy leader has explained our strategy to wrest the kingdom from the hands of Emmanuel by capturing the hearts of his subjects. Allow me to present the first phase in that strategy."

Captain Pleasure raised his hands high overhead and brought them down in a forceful, dramatic gesture. An immense puff of smoke filled the stage. As the smoke began to dissipate, a murmur of astonishment swept across the crowd. An enormous crystal sphere fully eighteen feet tall had appeared in the center of the stage! "Lords and ladies of the realm of darkness," Captain Pleasure cried, "behold Argamor's first weapon in the battle to steal the hearts of the men of Terrestria from their King!"

"It's the spellavision!" Josiah exclaimed in astonishment.

"The what?" Selwyn demanded.

"The spellavision," the young prince repeated. "The Countess of Covetousness tried to use it to place me under her spell when I was on my way to the Castle of Godliness. She had one that was much smaller, of course, but I am certain that it was the very same thing."

Captain Pleasure waved his hands again, and the image of a glittering castle of gold appeared inside the giant crystal sphere. Exclamations of amazement and awe echoed across the vast underground chamber. As the crowd watched in spellbound silence, a knight mounted on a handsome black charger came thundering across the castle drawbridge and galloped at full speed along a dusty road. The image of the galloping horse and rider sped past a backdrop of brilliant green forests, thundering waterfalls white with spray, majestic purple mountains, and sapphire blue lakes. The enchanting images appeared and disappeared to the accompaniment of stirring music that filled the amphitheater and overwhelmed the senses. The warriors were mesmerized.

Reining his horse to an abrupt halt, the knight within the sphere dismounted and drew his sword. Holding the weapon high in the air, he advanced toward a dark cave in the side of a steep mountain. A thunderous roar shook the amphitheater as a huge, fire-breathing dragon exploded into view from the mouth of the cave. The knight ran forward, shouting fiercely as he brandished his sword.

At that moment, the images in the giant sphere seemed to freeze in place as all motion suddenly ceased. The charging dragon stood transfixed with a plume of flame suspended in front of his nostrils. The knight hung motionless in mid-stride, both feet off the ground, sword raised but unmoving. Time stood still. The crowd waited in breathless anticipation. "Continue! Continue! Continue!" they began to chant, throwing dark looks of irritation at Captain Pleasure.

The huge crystal sphere began to flash with brilliantly colored images, drawing the crowd's attention back to it like a magnet. Glittering visions of castles and lands and rich clothing and beautiful women and smartly dressed servants and horses and carriages appeared and disappeared within the sphere almost faster than the eye could follow. Majestic music poured from the sphere, filling the amphitheater with overwhelming sound as the brilliant visual images captivated the thousands who watched. Suddenly the crystal sphere turned dark and the music ceased. An audible groan went up from the crowd.

Captain Pleasure laughed. "You have just witnessed the power of a delightful device called 'spellavision'. As you have seen, your attention was captivated at once by the colorful images that appear and disappear so easily within the crystal. It will be the same with those who are loyal to Emmanuel—we will captivate their minds with the spellavision and use it to steal their hearts from their King."

He grinned evilly. "Here is our strategy: we plan to place a spellavision—smaller than this one, of course—in the center of every home in Terrestria. Every home in the kingdom, from the richest castle of the greatest nobleman to the humblest cottage of the poorest peasant, will soon boast one of these enchanting inventions. We will employ the most capable writers in the kingdom to script dramas and plays and vignettes to entertain the populace. We will call these performances 'programs', but they will contain far more than mere entertainment. Through these programs, we will place Emmanuel's subjects under a spell and then steal their hearts. We will teach them to tolerate evil, and then eventually, to embrace it. The spellavision will teach them to laugh at, and then eventually participate in, that which is shameful and vulgar and blasphemous. Through clever writing, captivating drama, and irresistible music, we shall cause them to love the very things that Emmanuel hates. The spellavision will be especially effective in taking Argamor's message to the younger subjects of the kingdom; we shall teach them to be rebellious, immoral, selfish, dishonest and disloyal, and they will never realize what we are doing to them!"

Spontaneous applause broke out in one corner of the great amphitheater and then spread across the crowd like wildfire. Cheers and shouting echoed across the vast assembly.

When the excitement had died down, a warrior on the front row of the amphitheater rose to his feet. "I see only one flaw in your grand scheme, Captain," he called. "The followers of Emmanuel will never allow this enchanting creation of yours into their homes. Once they learn that we are using this device to present Argamor's philosophies and corrupt their hearts—and the hearts of their children—they will reject the spellavision as if it were the purveyor of a plague!"

Captain Pleasure laughed, and the sound echoed throughout Lower Terrestria. "Oh, but that's where you are mistaken, my friend. Not only will they *allow* it, they will *welcome* it!"

"Nay, I still say that they will refuse anything that contradicts the will of their King," the challenger insisted. "Any loyal follower of Emmanuel will reject the spellavision. The images that have danced before our eyes these past few moments were fascinating, to be sure, but Emmanuel's subjects will see through your scheme."

"We have planned this well, my friend," the tall warlord replied. "Our programs at first will be simple and entertaining, and relatively innocent. Very little of Argamor's message will be presented when the spellavision is first introduced. But as time goes by and the populace has become accustomed to seeing it in their homes, we will introduce more and more that is evil. The message of Argamor will become bolder, and the programs will contain much that speaks to the evil nature of the people. In time, they will accept almost anything in the name of education and entertainment."

Argamor spoke up. "Captain Pleasure is right," he asserted. "A live frog placed in a boiling pot will immediately leap to safety; but a frog placed in a pot of cool water that is gradually heated to a boil will stay and simmer to his death. We will move so slowly and present our message with such subtlety that Emmanuel's most loyal subjects will be unaware of what we are doing. The stealing of hearts by means of the spellavision will take place gradually."

"Thank you, my lord," Captain Pleasure said, flashing a grateful smile in Argamor's direction.

He turned to the crowd. "There is a second phase to my part of the plan to steal the hearts of Emmanuel's subjects," he announced. Again he raised his hands high overhead and brought them down in a dramatic gesture. The enormous spellavision disappeared in a puff of smoke; in its place stood four minstrels dressed in black robes. Three of them held stringed instruments of various designs; the fourth stood behind a collection of large rocks arranged in a semicircle around him. Holding two polished wooden sticks, he commenced beating a staccato rhythm on the rocks. The other three musicians began to strum their instruments furiously, and all four began to weave and gyrate wildly. The result was a deafening cacophony of discordant sound that filled the vast amphitheater with a pulsating rhythm, echoing back and forth across Lower Terrestria until it reached a painful crescendo. The vast throng of robed figures leaped to their feet and began to sway and gyrate in synchronization with the pounding rhythm.

Josiah and Selwyn covered their ears, grimacing in displeasure. "What an appalling noise," Josiah said to Selwyn. "I can actually feel it inside my head!"

"Aye," Selwyn replied, "it is so loud that it causes me pain!"

The four gyrating minstrels stopped abruptly and stood motionless. The earsplitting noise echoed across the cavern for a few seconds and then died out. The boys both let out sighs of relief.

"Our Lord and Master's own music," Captain Pleasure said proudly, "the music of the stones. As you know, Lord Argamor himself designed this music to extend his influence over Terrestria. I am pleased to announce that he has chosen at this time to introduce this music throughout the kingdom. Soon we shall have many of the kingdom's minstrels and troubadours performing this music in the hamlets and villages and cities, the cottages and the courts and the castles.

"As this music spreads across the kingdom like a rain cloud moving across a wheat field, Argamor's message and influence will spread and increase. The stone music is yet another tool that we shall use to capture the hearts and minds of Emmanuel's followers.

"I'm sure that you realize that music was originally designed by our adversary, Emmanuel. He has used it as a powerful weapon for good. Argamor has taken this weapon, changed it, and turned it into a powerful weapon for evil. When we introduce the stone music to the inhabitants of Terrestria, it will contain messages of rebellion, selfishness, deceit, immorality, and even self-destruction. We plan to present it as the music of youth in order that this message will reach the hearts of Emmanuel's youngest followers."

Captain Pleasure suddenly grinned. "Fellow subjects of Argamor, you could say that our master has stolen a weapon from Emmanuel and turned it against him!" Ripples of laughter spread across the throng, followed by applause and then shouts of victory. Thousands stood to their feet and cheered wildly for nearly two minutes. At a gesture from Captain Pleasure, they took their seats and grew quiet.

"Captain Pleasure, I again see a problem with your clever scheme to introduce the music of the stones to the loyal followers of Emmanuel." All eyes darted to the front row of the amphitheater. The knight who had challenged the effectiveness of the spellavision was again standing on his feet. "If this music contains words that are openly evil, will it not be rejected by those who are loyal to our adversary, Emmanuel?" The warrior sat back down.

"That is a good question, my friend," Captain Pleasure replied pleasantly. "There are those among Emmanuel's subjects whose hearts are not yielded to their King, and they will accept this music immediately. Then there are those, of course, among his subjects who are alert and discerning. They will immediately reject the music of the stones and caution others among them to do the same. Still others will be attracted to this music, but will be cautious simply because it is new and different.

"We will introduce stone music that mentions Emmanuel's name and presents just enough of his truth to sound convincing. Once we have those subjects listening to this music, we can soon convince them to listen to any music that we want."

At a gesture from the captain, the four minstrels began to play again, and the discordant sound again filled the amphitheater. "Why do they call it music?" Josiah complained. "It's mostly just rhythm and noise."

Captain Pleasure lifted his hands and brought them down in a quick slashing motion. The minstrels disappeared in a puff of smoke and the sounds of their frenzied efforts died out. Silence reigned momentarily, and the two young princes were relieved. Captain Pleasure turned and bowed to Argamor. "There you have it, my Lord: my part of the strategy to steal the hearts of Emmanuel's most loyal subjects."

The captain turned and walked back to his seat to a round of thunderous applause. Beaming proudly, he sat down once again behind the council fire. Argamor strode to center stage. The applause died down, and silence prevailed.

"My loyal subjects, lords and ladies of the realm of darkness," the powerful warlord began, "Captain Pleasure is but one member of the Council of Six. You have heard but one part of our battle strategy. The others will soon present their various phases of the strategy.

"Judge for yourselves—will this campaign to steal the hearts of the kingdom be victorious? Will we succeed in our efforts to dethrone Emmanuel?"

The entire throng of dark knights leaped to their feet. The sounds of their cheering and the rattle of their swords echoed across Lower Terrestria. Selwyn turned to Josiah. "Let's get out of here and make our journey back to the Castle of Faith."

Josiah grabbed his arm. "Nay, Selwyn, we must stay. I also want to leave, but someone must be here to hear the rest. We must know what Argamor and his evil forces have planned for Terrestria in order that we might be prepared to resist."

Chapter Twelve

"The next member of the Council of Six," Argamor announced grandly, "is Captain Discontent." A polite ripple of applause swept briefly across the amphitheater and then quickly died out. Argamor turned. "Captain."

One of the warlords arose from one of the great chairs and strode quickly forward. "My ladies and lords, servants to Lord Argamor," Captain Discontent began, and Josiah was surprised to realize that the warlord was a woman. The voice was hard and masculine, harsh in tone and powerful in volume, but the speaker was unmistakably a woman. "Lord Argamor has asked me to present my phase of our strategy in the battle for the kingdom of Terrestria. The strategy that I am about to propose can become a powerful and effective weapon in our quest for the hearts and minds of Emmanuel's followers. Please harken carefully to what I have to say."

Captain Discontent paused for a moment; her gaze swept across the sea of faces before her. The vast throng of dark knights waited expectantly.

"Look at the coat of arms on her shield," Selwyn whispered. "What an unusual symbol: a circle with an upside down cross hanging from it! What do you suppose that means?"

Josiah shrugged. "I have no idea."

"Our plan," Captain Discontent announced, "is to cause the women of Emmanuel's kingdom to become dissatisfied with their lot in life. We must tell them that they have been oppressed and downtrodden by the men of the kingdom, and by Emmanuel himself. We must convince them that the roles their King has planned for them are subservient to the roles that he has for the men; we must deceive them into thinking that they are little more than slaves. We must make them think that they are looked upon with disdain and disfavor because they are women.

"We shall tell them over and over that obedience to their husbands is nothing more than primitive servitude, that their King has deliberately placed them in positions that demean and debase them. We shall employ the use of Captain Pleasure's spellavision and his music of the stones to spread our message. Every troubadour who travels from castle to castle will tell stories that develop this idea, as well as sing ballads that reinforce it. If the women of the kingdom hear this theme over and over, they will begin to believe it. They will then begin to distrust Emmanuel."

The captain paused again. She had noticed that the crowd was silent; her words were not being received with the same enthusiasm that Captain Pleasure's plan had enjoyed. She cleared her throat and continued. "Once we have convinced the female members of the kingdom that their King has placed them in a position that suggests inferiority, a lowly position that is little more than servitude, we can cause them to rebel against Emmanuel's plan for them. They will rebel against their husbands. Under the banner of better treatment and equality, they will demand positions of leadership in their homes and towns and castles."

The vast amphitheater was quiet as Captain Discontent swept the crowd with a measuring glance as she attempted to determine the effect of her words. She realized that her message was not being received with enthusiasm. A thoughtful look appeared on her rugged face. She paused, and then, in a moment of decision, turned to Captain Pleasure. "My lord, would you allow me the use of your spellavision?"

Captain Pleasure bowed. "Certainly, my lady. My pleasure." He rose from his chair, lifted his hands, and then brought them down quickly and forcefully. In a billowing puff of smoke, the huge crystal sphere reappeared in the center of the stage.

Captain Discontent stepped close to the spellavision and clapped her hands three times. Instantly, the image of a peasant woman fifteen feet tall appeared within the crystal. Her long, blonde hair glistened like spun gold against the fabric of her simple peasant gown. Her face was simple, her eyes trusting, and her expression serene. She held a milk pail in her left hand.

Captain Discontent raised her hand and gestured toward the image in the spellavision. "Here is the typical woman in Emmanuel's kingdom: simple-minded, compliant, content with her insignificant lot in life as assigned her by her King. She has been told that she must ride sidesaddle, that she must obey her husband, that she must not have a voice in the affairs of the kingdom. Ladies and lords of the realm of darkness, we must change that!"

Again the female warlord clapped her hands three times. In an instant, the image within the crystal sphere changed to that of a female warrior in armor, with a sword in her right hand and a helmet held in the crook of her left arm. The long, golden hair told Josiah that this was the same woman, but now there was a vast difference: her face was hard, her eyes belligerent, and her expression cold and hateful.

Captain Discontent's masculine face wore a look of proud accomplishment as she gestured toward the image in the spellavision. "Here is the model woman that we want the women of the kingdom to emulate: aggressive and assertive, determined and domineering, dissatisfied with the role assigned to her, and willing to do whatever it takes to change it. This woman, free to choose her own destiny and willing to fight for fulfillment, will no longer ride sidesaddle. She will ride astride a horse like a man. She will no longer listen to her husband; in fact, she will tell him what to do. She will raise her voice with the voices of other women who have been liberated from Emmanuel's tyranny whenever she thinks that she is not getting her way. This woman, no longer content to help, will seek positions of power and prestige."

Captain Discontent paused as if expecting a show of approval from the vast throng in the amphitheater, but instead, there was an intense silence. Nobody stirred; nobody moved. The captain nervously cleared her throat. "And there you have my strategy for capturing the hearts of the kingdom."

There was movement on the front row, and all eyes turned in that direction. The now familiar challenger was standing. "My lady, I fail to see the significance of your plan. We are discussing strategy to overthrow the kingdom and place Argamor on the throne, and yet you are talking about whether or not a woman should ride sidesaddle! What difference does it make? Even if we could create discontent in the heart of every female in Emmanuel's kingdom, what would we have accomplished? We are here to discuss strategy to seize a kingdom, not decide whether or not women should ride sidesaddle!" The knight sat back down.

A murmur of agreement swept across the vast audience. It was obvious that the entire crowd favored the challenger's reasoning and that they were ready to dismiss Captain Discontent's strategy as irrelevant. The vast throng buzzed with commotion as the members of the audience discussed the captain's plan. Josiah heard a few snickers here and there, and then ripples of laughter.

Captain Discontent stood in front of the spellavision, angry and defiant, as she watched the reaction to the strategy that she had just presented. "My fellow ladies and lords," she cried, "give my plan your consideration!" But the laughter increased in volume.

With a snort of indignation, Argamor bounded to the center of the stage. "Fools!" he raged, growing red in the face. The laughter died like a burning ember dropped into a bucket of water. Argamor turned and spat on the stage in disgust. "Fools, every one of you! Fools and idiots and buffoons! At the moment, I am ashamed to call you my followers. Is the whole lot of you this dull, this dim-witted?"

The throng sat silent, embarrassed and cowed like a group of whipped puppies before their master. An atmosphere of tense discomfort hung over the amphitheater.

"Captain Discontent has just unveiled a remarkable strategy," the powerful warlord raged, "and yet you have jeered and laughed at her. Fools! Idiots and buffoons, every one of you!" He turned to the warlord. "Excellent presentation, Captain. Your strategy is subtle, yet powerful, and the possibilities are incredible. The tactics that you have just outlined will be invaluable in our quest to wrest the kingdom from Emmanuel."

Argamor turned back to the crowd, spreading his arms wide as if to make an appeal. "My lords and ladies of the dark realm, can you not see the possibilities behind Captain Discontent's strategy? Are you too dull, too dim-witted, too muddle-headed to imagine what this could do for our campaign to seize the throne? Think with me, my lords and ladies! Emmanuel has decreed that the men of the kingdom shall be the leaders in their homes. He has decreed that they shall be the leaders in the castles. Furthermore, he has decreed that the women of his kingdom are to have a meek and quiet spirit. My devoted disciples, remember this—half of Emmanuel's followers are female! If we can convince the women of the kingdom to go against Emmanuel's orders and become the aggressive women that Captain Discontent has described, fully half of the kingdom is then in rebellion against their King. Without even realizing it, they will have opened their hearts to our plan and our influence.

"The women of the kingdom are far more important than you apparently realize. There are times when a woman can be more effective for evil than a man. An Eve is oftentimes a greater weapon in my hands than an Adam. There are times when I can use a Jezebel more effectively than I can use an Ahab.

"Furthermore, when a woman does not follow her husband, her rebellion encourages rebellion in her children. They will rebel against their parents and against their King simply because they have seen rebellion in the heart of their mother. Lords and ladies, Captain Discontent has just given us a powerful strategy that will enable us to capture the hearts of the youth of the kingdom!

"Resentment will build between husbands and wives, and families will be weakened as a result. When we weaken the families, we weaken the kingdom! Victory is then just around the corner."

He turned and looked at Captain Discontent. "Well done, Captain! That was an excellent presentation. I believe that your strategy will be far more effective than any of us can now visualize. Your plan will have a tremendous impact against the kingdom of Emmanuel. The realm of darkness thanks you, Captain."

The captain bowed to Argamor. Sweeping the darkened amphitheater with a satisfied smirk of triumph, she walked back to her seat behind the blazing fire pit. There was a moment of intense silence, and then the vast amphitheater suddenly erupted with enthusiastic applause.

Chapter Thirteen

"The next member of the Council of Six to present his strategy," Argamor announced to the thousands seated before him, "will be Captain Covetous. Lords and ladies of the realm of darkness, please welcome this stalwart officer!" Polite applause rippled across the amphitheater.

A short, stocky little warlord arose from his seat behind the fire pit and walked forward. Josiah noticed that his armor glistened with a strange green hue. His helmet, his breastplate, his sword and his shield all glittered with countless jewels. A rainbow of color and light shimmered around him and every move he made was accented with flashes of colored fire from the sparkling gems. The coat of arms on his shield was simple: a treasure chest.

"My lords and my ladies," Captain Covetous began, in a whiny voice that set Josiah's nerves on edge, "the two stalwart captains before me have presented excellent strategies for the advancement of Lord Argamor's evil kingdom. I am pleased to announce that my officers, Captain Greed, Captain Envious, Captain Desire, and Captain Lovemoney, have worked long and hard to develop yet another phase of the campaign to seize the throne for Lord Argamor. Please attend carefully as I outline our phase of the battle strategy.

"After long study of the inhabitants of Terrestria, my officers and I have come to the conclusion that most of Emmanuel's followers can still be tempted with promises of wealth and material possessions. They have an extreme fondness for riches. They become emotionally attached to their possessions, almost to the point of worship. They judge a man's worth by the amount of wealth and possessions that he has accumulated.

"We can conclude that they did not listen when their King told them that a man's life consists not in the abundance of the things that he possesses. Many of Emmanuel's followers are consumed with an undying passion to accumulate more wealth and possessions. Even when they reach the point where they have more than they could ever need they continue to scramble to accumulate more. Lords and ladies of the realm of darkness, we can capitalize on those weaknesses."

He turned and looked at Captain Pleasure. "My phase of the strategy will make use of your wondrous invention, the spellavision. Right now my men are busy writing performances—programs, I believe you called them—that will encourage Emmanuel's followers in this insatiable thirst for wealth. Using your wonderful spellavision, we plan to showcase the wealth of the kingdom with all of its castles and money and horses and clothing and carriages, in order that the populace may see that others have more than they do. In this way we will create within their hearts a desire to have more.

"We will also plan to communicate the philosophy that a person is a success in life only when he has more wealth and possessions than his neighbor. Thus, the people of the kingdom will be constantly striving for wealth as a matter of status. They will learn to resent those who have more than they do. Envy and jealousy will flourish. Those who have less than their neighbors will actually learn to resent and mistrust their King, as though he had not been fair with them.

"I would go so far as to predict that one day material gain will become so important that the women of the kingdom will leave their homes, abandoning their children to the care of others, in order to pursue wealth for their families. Perhaps Captain Discontent and her special forces can work on that angle for us."

Captain Covetous grinned evilly. His dark eyes glittered with anticipation. "As we see it, this strategy of ours will accomplish two principal purposes: first, it will focus the attention of Emmanuel's subjects on wealth and prosperity, rather than on righteousness, virtue, and service to their King. Their love for their King will shrivel and die. The pursuit of wealth will become their primary purpose in life.

"Second, the people of the kingdom will begin to place their trust in riches, rather than in Emmanuel. We will steal their hearts by transferring their love, their loyalties, and their trust from their King to their material possessions." He spread his arms wide. "And there, my lords and ladies, is an overview of our strategy to steal the hearts of the kingdom."

"I love it!" Argamor cried, leaping forward on the stage to slap Captain Covetous on the back. "Captain, you have served me well. Your part of the strategy to steal the hearts is tremendous."

Captain Covetous smiled. "My men and I are happy to be of service, my lord. By serving you we strike a blow against our enemy, Emmanuel, and we are always eager to do that."

The crowd applauded as the captain returned to his seat.

Captain Confusion, a tall, slender man, jittery with nervous energy, was the next of Argamor's warlords to present a strategy in the battle for men's hearts. His face was pale as he walked forward to address the vast throng, and his eyes darted constantly from place to place as if he were searching for an avenue of escape. "Lords and ladies of the dark realm," he began, and his voice cracked. The audience tittered nervously.

"My strategy for stealing the hearts of the kingdom is quite simple," the tall warlord continued. He clasped and unclasped his hands constantly as he talked, and he nervously shifted his weight from side to side. "We plan to get Emmanuel's subjects so busy with activity that they no longer have time to think about their King, much less serve him. We will get them to crowd their schedules with innocent but worthless activities. As they become busier and busier, rushing about from one urgent pastime to another, their King will be forgotten. Their love for him will grow cold like a pot of forgotten porridge."

As he talked, Captain Confusion's hands were never still. They flailed the air in meaningless gestures, clasped and unclasped repeatedly, or fidgeted with the fastenings on his breastplate. It was as if he simply did not know what to do with them. "My officers and I are working on a particular diversion that should be quite successful in drawing the attention of the populace away from their King." Reaching up over his head, he seemed to pull a small, white sphere out of the air. He cradled it in his hand. "Lords and ladies, do you know what this is?"

"It is a sphere," several voices called.

"Quite true," Captain Confusion replied, caressing the object and shifting it from hand to hand. "But this little sphere, called

a 'ball' by the inhabitants of Terrestria, has some excellent possibilities for our campaign. As you know, many of the populace
are quite competitive. They love a contest, whether it be one of
strength, wits, or skill. We plan to encourage them to develop
competitions between themselves. The possibilities are limitless. Take this sphere, for instance. A sphere such as this one
could be hit with a stick for sport."

The sphere in his hands suddenly turned brown and swelled
until it was many times its original size. "If we increase its size,
it could be bounced on the floor and thrown through large
hoops suspended on the wall."

Holding his hands on each side of the sphere, the fidgety
warlord brought his fingers toward one another and then drew
his hands apart. The sphere assumed an unusual oblong shape.
"If we modify it slightly, like this, it can be passed through the
air or kicked with the foot." As he spoke, the oblong shape
abruptly turned white, became a perfect sphere again, and
shrank rapidly until it was barely the size of a walnut. "It could
even be struck with a club and driven into holes in the ground.
As I said, the possibilities are endless.

"The point is this—we will put such a huge emphasis on the
various games that can be played with these clever little spheres
that Emmanuel's people will begin to neglect their duties to
their King, in order that they might participate in these games.
The games in themselves, mind you, will be quite innocent. If
held in their proper place, they could actually be quite whole-
some. But we believe that we can appeal to the competitive
nature of the populace and cause them to make these harm-
less pastimes a priority. As a result, their loyalty and love for
Emmanuel will suffer. The men of the kingdom will be especially susceptible, but many of the women will be drawn in, too."

Captain Confusion grinned and turned to Captain Pleasure. "We also plan to make use of your magnificent spellavision. We will display games of competition at regular intervals. Those of the kingdom who are not agile enough to participate in actual competition can watch others compete, and thus they will still be drawn into this diversion. If this proves to be as effective as we anticipate, these competitions might in time actually become more important to these spectators than service to their King. Incredible as it seems, we have reason to believe that it will work."

Captain Confusion smiled, still clasping and unclasping his hands. "My whole strategy comes down to this one simple idea: one way or another, we plan to keep the people so busy with activities, some good and some bad, that they simply will have no time to praise and serve their King."

He looked at Captain Covetous. "There is one aspect of your strategy that we plan to develop, Captain. You plan to steal the people's hearts by persuading them to acquire more and more possessions. With the increase in possessions comes an increase in activity and responsibility. A man who owns a horse must take care of it. A man who owns a cottage must maintain it. So as you steal their hearts with increased possessions, you also burden them down with increased responsibilities, thus keeping them too busy to serve Emmanuel.

"Lords and ladies, you have my strategy." Captain Confusion drew a polite round of applause as he walked back to his seat.

To Josiah's surprise, the last two warlords stepped forward together to address the vast throng of evil warriors. Captain Despair was a heavyset man with a broad, red face and tiny, shifty eyes that held a look of hopelessness; his companion,

Captain Apathy, was small, with thin features and a dark complexion. Captain Despair was the first to speak. "My forces and I have arrived at a strategy to demoralize Emmanuel's followers," he announced. "One of the most effective weapons in Argamor's arsenal is the weapon of discouragement. A discouraged foe is a defeated foe."

He grinned evilly as he paused and scanned his audience. The vast throng of dark warriors waited expectantly. "Our strategy is simple. We have a massive propaganda scheme in place to spread the lie that Argamor is in a greater position of power than Emmanuel— that the kingdom of Terrestria is about to fall to our master. We will do everything we can to convince Emmanuel's followers that Terrestria is being overrun by the forces of evil, that there is no hope for righteousness and virtue.

"Using Captain Pleasure's magnificent spellavision, we plan to publicize every evil deed that we possibly can. Each time a man or woman within the kingdom commits an evil deed, we will turn it into a little victory for evil. We will announce it publicly and get people talking about it. If the evildoer is one of Emmanuel's loyal followers, the victory will be even sweeter, and we will publicize it all the more. We want to create the impression that evil is triumphing, that good is being defeated.

"The end result will be that Emmanuel's followers will become convinced that they are on the losing side, that the evil forces of Argamor are winning the kingdom. Discouragement among Emmanuel's ranks is sure to follow. And as I pointed out already, a discouraged foe is a defeated foe." He turned and glanced at his companion, Captain Apathy.

"Thank you, Captain," the swarthy little warlord said. He turned and addressed the crowd. "Once Captain Despair and his capable forces have spread their message of doom and gloom, an atmosphere of hopelessness will pervade within Emmanuel's kingdom. My forces will then move in. Discouragement can quickly be turned to apathy. A man who is defeated in mind and spirit is easily defeated in battle, for he no longer has the heart to fight for his King. Once my worthy colleague has convinced Emmanuel's followers that they have no hope of victory and that evil is triumphing, they will quickly lose heart. They will decide that it no longer matters whether or not they serve their King, since all is lost anyway."

The little captain smiled smugly. "My lords and ladies, as loyal warriors to the mighty Argamor, surely you can visualize what this will mean for our side. The battle will be won almost before we start to fight! Lord Argamor will prevail, and the kingdom will be ours. As Captain Despair has reminded us, a discouraged foe is a defeated foe. My lords and ladies, there you have it—my strategy for conquering the hearts of Emmanuel's followers."

As Captain Apathy turned and walked back to his seat, Argamor bounded forward with a look of evil triumph on his cruel features. "My lords and ladies, loyal servants of evil, warriors of the kingdom of darkness, Terrestria will soon be ours! The Council of Six have spoken; you have heard their wicked strategies. Together we shall seize Emmanuel's throne by winning the hearts of his followers. We shall not storm his castles nor march against his armies—we shall simply steal the heart of every man, woman, and child within the kingdom, and then, Terrestria is ours!"

The vast throng of evil warriors leaped to their feet, brandishing their weapons and shouting until the walls of the cavern shook with the force of the sound. On stage, the fire blazed so high that the flames touched the rocky ceiling of the enormous cavern. A rumbling roar like thunder swept across Lower Terrestria, growing louder and louder until the boys covered their ears and grimaced in pain. The ring of huge boulders trembled.

Selwyn's eyes were wide with fright. "It's an earthquake! We must get out of here!"

Josiah shook his head. "I don't think so. I think it's the forces of evil present in this room. We must stay and listen."

Argamor abruptly raised both hands and an unearthly silence settled across the amphitheater. The vast throng sank quietly to their seats. "Emmanuel's kingdom of righteousness and truth will fall. Argamor's kingdom of evil and darkness will prevail. My lords and ladies, the victory is ours!" The thousands of warriors in dark armor were instantly on their feet again, cheering and chanting and leaping about in their exuberance. Josiah shuddered as an incredible sensation of evil swept across the amphitheater.

Argamor waited, an evil smirk upon his fiendish face, as the tumult grew louder. When the frenzied display had reached a point where Josiah didn't think he could stand another moment, the burly warlord raised his hands and silence again prevailed. "You have noticed, I am sure," Argamor continued, "how the various strategies as presented by the Council of Six work together to bring about the downfall of our adversary's kingdom. The victory will not be won in a day, or even in a month or a year. We will proceed slowly, quietly winning one heart at a time. But be assured of this one thing—the victory will be ours!"

The vast throng started to leap to their feet again at this point, but their leader quelled them with one gesture of his huge hands. "Today the Council of Six have presented the basic components of our strategy. There are, of course, other details of strategy that have not been discussed here. In the days ahead, your commanding officers will keep you informed of these other details. They will also present your individual assignments in this important campaign. My lords and ladies, congratulate yourselves for choosing the winning side! I thank each of you for your commitment to our evil cause."

As the vast throng leaped again to their feet, Selwyn turned to Josiah. "He's getting ready to dismiss this assembly. Let's get out of here before we're discovered!"

Josiah frowned as he turned to follow his companion back up the winding lane that led from the underground city. "Argamor didn't even mention the Crown of Kuros," he muttered, "and neither did any of his warlords. I wonder why."

At that moment, two dark forms moved from the shadows and leaped into the center of the lane, blocking the path of the two young princes. Arcs of blue light slashed across the darkness as the two figures whisked light wands from behind their backs. Terror seized Josiah when he realized that he and Selwyn were face to face with two of Argamor's burly sentries. "Intruders!" one of the guards growled, drawing his sword. "Perchance they are spies for Emmanuel. Seize them!"

Chapter Fourteen

Argamor's guards advanced slowly, menacingly, with glowing light wands in their left hands and swords in their right. The polished steel blades reflected the soft blue light, giving them an ominous, unearthly appearance. Prince Josiah felt a surge of panic.

"Aye, Depravity," one of the sentries growled to his companion, "I believe that you are right—we *have* caught two of Emmanuel's spies. Shall we kill them or take them alive?"

"Neither," Prince Josiah shouted, "for we are indeed servants to King Emmanuel, and we fight in the power of his name!" Pulling the book from his doublet, he swung it fiercely, and the invincible blade seemed to glow with a light of its own as it sliced through the air. Prince Selwyn drew his sword an instant later, and both young princes rushed headlong at the menacing guards.

Josiah's sword hummed as the young prince attacked the evil guard closest to him, swinging the weapon overhead with both hands. The man stepped backwards, getting his own blade up just in the nick of time to fend off the mighty blow. Josiah swung the powerful weapon furiously, slashing and cutting and thrusting as he pressed forward. His opponent struggled to defend himself. Selwyn was shoulder to shoulder with Josiah, attacking with a fury equal to Josiah's. Caught off guard, Argamor's two men fell back before the furious onslaught of the two young princes. Within moments, both evil guards lay dead upon the ground.

"Victory is ours, Josiah," Selwyn exulted. "But we had better make ourselves scarce before we have to face that mob in the amphitheater!" Holding their swords at the ready, the two young princes sprinted for the soft blue light of the tunnel entrance.

"How do we get out?" Selwyn asked in bewilderment as they reached the upper end of the glowing tunnel and found themselves facing a solid wall of rock. Sword in hand, he spun around and assumed a fighting stance, as if expecting to find Argamor's hordes pursuing him.

"I would imagine that we get out the same way we got in," Josiah replied. Transferring his sword to his left hand, he reached up with his right and knocked on the rock wall six times. He paused, knocked six more times, paused, and then rapped again six times. Just as he expected, the wall opened with a soft whooshing sound. A sense of relief swept over him as he and Selwyn stepped through the remarkable doorway.

"Look, it has stopped raining," Selwyn observed as he and Josiah hurried to their horses. "That was a quick storm."

"How long do you think we were in Lower Terrestria?" Josiah asked. "We may have been down there longer than we realized. Look, the sun has already set. It will be completely dark in less than half an hour."

"Let's ride swiftly for home," Selwyn suggested. The two young princes hastily untied their mounts and swung into the saddles. As they rode from beneath the gigantic overhang of granite, both were thinking of Argamor's council of war that they had just witnessed. Josiah shuddered.

Twenty minutes later, Selwyn drew back on the reins. "Perhaps we should stop somewhere for the night," he said in a quiet voice. "It's getting so dark that I can hardly see my horse's ears."

"Our books will lead us," Josiah replied. "We need to put as much distance between us and Lower Terrestria as possible." He glanced around. Selwyn was right—the woods through which they were riding were dark. Just then, he spotted a faint gleam of flickering light through the trees to the right of the trail. "Look! A campfire!"

"Let's investigate it, but we need to approach slowly," Selwyn cautioned. "It might be some of Argamor's men."

"Why would they camp out this close to the entrance to Lower Terrestria?" Josiah responded. Nevertheless, he found that his heart pounded faster.

Dismounting, the two young princes tied their horses to a tree and then crept cautiously toward the flickering light, doing their best to move quietly through the carpet of brown leaves covering the ground. Slipping furtively down the side of a rocky, tree-shrouded slope, they soon found a small campfire burning brightly in a clearing at the base of the hill. Holding a finger to his lips, Josiah crept closer.

Thirty feet from the campfire, the two young princes crouched behind the broad trunk of an enormous oak. "Can you see anyone?" Josiah whispered to Selwyn, who peered cautiously around the trunk. Selwyn glanced at Josiah and shook his head.

"Come out, lads," an amused voice called. "I know you're there."

Hearts pounding with fear, the two young princes stepped from behind the tree, drawing their swords as they did. To Josiah's immense relief, an old man with friendly gray eyes was waiting for them. "Sir Wisdom!" Josiah exclaimed. "Sire, I'm so glad it is you!"

Sir Wisdom spread his arms wide in a gesture of welcome. "Josiah, my prince, how are you? Selwyn, it is so good to see you."

"Sir Wisdom has always been a real encouragement to me," Josiah said, turning to Selwyn. "He helped me on my quest to the seven castles."

His companion nodded. "I made the journey to the same seven castles, remember? Sir Wisdom aided me, too. We know each other well."

"Dinner is almost ready, lads. I'm serving roast pheasant. Find a dry spot on the log there by the fire and get warm." Josiah stepped close to the crackling fire and held his hands out over the flames. The warmth from the fire felt good.

"I'll get the horses." Selwyn started off through the woods.

Josiah dropped gratefully to a seat on the log. Sir Wisdom knelt and rotated a spit suspended over the fire. The fire crackled and popped as the juices from two golden brown roasting birds dripped into the flames. A delicious aroma filled the air. "Sire," Josiah said hesitantly, "Selwyn and I just came from a place called Lower Terrestria."

The old man nodded knowingly. "The underground city. You eavesdropped on Argamor's council of war."

The young prince was startled almost beyond words. "Sire, how did you know?"

Sir Wisdom laughed. "I make it my business to know these things, lad."

Josiah shook his head in amazement. "Six of Argamor's most powerful warlords were there, sire. They were called the Council of Six. They presented strategies to seize the throne from His Majesty, King Emmanuel, and take over the kingdom." He gazed earnestly at Sir Wisdom. "Do you know what they plan to do, sire? They plan to take the kingdom one heart at a time! Argamor said that they will not march against King Emmanuel's armies or attack his castles; instead, they will attack the individual members of the kingdom and steal their hearts from Emmanuel. Is that possible, sire?"

Sir Wisdom looked up from the roasting pheasants. "Aye, lad, it is."

"Each of Argamor's warlords presented a different part of the strategy to win the kingdom," Josiah continued. Briefly, he recounted the various plans that the Council of Six had presented. "It was frightening, sire. As they talked, I could feel the very presence of evil in the amphitheater. The only reason we stayed was so that we could listen and then report their evil strategies to King Emmanuel. Sire, we need to send a messenger to the Golden City. King Emmanuel must be told of Argamor's plans to seize the throne!"

The old man chuckled. "He knows every detail, my prince."

"Does he know about the various strategies that Argamor's warlords plan to use?"

"Aye, he knows everything. He knows every detail of the plans being hatched by Argamor and his warlords. You see, Josiah, your King is aware of everything that takes place within his kingdom. Never has a sparrow fallen to the ground but that His Majesty knew about it."

Josiah gave voice to a fear that was troubling him. "Argamor is determined, sire. His warlords are crafty and his warriors are numerous. Their strategies are well-planned. What if... what if they are victorious? What if Argamor is able to seize King Emmanuel's throne? What will happen then?"

The old nobleman laughed gently. "Josiah, Josiah. That will never happen. No one will overthrow King Emmanuel, not even Argamor and all his evil forces. Emmanuel is sovereign and his throne is invincible. His kingdom is forever. Never will there be a warlord powerful enough nor an army big enough to take his throne." He shook his head. "Nay, lad, you need not worry about Argamor seizing Emmanuel's throne!"

"But what if it happens?" the young prince argued. "You seem so sure, but what if it happens? What if Argamor and his huge army of evil warriors do win this battle and wrest the throne from Emmanuel?"

Sir Wisdom stooped and picked up an acorn from the ground. "Come with me, Prince Josiah." The young prince followed the nobleman through the woods. Within moments they came to a clearing. "Look yonder," Sir Wisdom urged. "What do you see?"

Josiah stared. "Where? I don't see anything."

"High in the heavens," the old man coaxed, pointing. "Don't you see it, way up there above us?"

"The moon?"

"Nay, not the moon." Sir Wisdom was patient. He pointed again. "Don't you see it, lad? A tiny dark speck, high above us, soaring across the heavens…"

Josiah studied the starry sky but still didn't see anything.

Sir Wisdom leaned closer as he pointed. "Watch the moon," he urged. "Here it comes… now! Do you see it?"

As Josiah watched, a tiny object crossed in front of the moon, a black silhouette against the bright silver orb. An instant later it had crossed the moon and was now dark and indistinct against the velvety sky but the young prince continued to track it with his eye as it soared across the heavens. "What is it, sire?"

"An eagle. A golden eagle."

"An eagle?" Josiah echoed. "But it's so small!"

"That eagle has a seven-foot wingspan," the old man replied, "but it's at least a thousand feet in the air." He handed Josiah the acorn he had picked up at the campfire. "Here. Take this, my prince, and use it to knock the eagle from the skies."

"I beg your pardon, sire?"

"Throw the acorn at the eagle," Sir Wisdom repeated. "See if you can bring the eagle down."

Josiah laughed in confusion. "That's—that's preposterous, sire! If the eagle is a thousand feet in the air, I could never hit it from here! And even if I could, the acorn would not harm the eagle. What you're asking is impossible, sire."

"But what if you *can* knock the eagle down with an acorn?" the old man persisted. "You seem so sure that you cannot, but what if you can? Why not at least try?"

Josiah frowned. "Why are you asking me to try this, sire? It is impossible! It is absurd! No one can bring an eagle down from a thousand feet with an acorn!"

"Imagine a little gray squirrel scampering one day through the forest," Sir Wisdom said softly. "He looks up and sees that eagle soaring so majestically through the heavens, and his little heart becomes extremely jealous. He gathers a pile of acorns and begins to hurl them towards the heavens in hopes of knocking that mighty eagle from the skies. What do you think are his chances of success?"

Josiah laughed. "It would be impossible, sire. A squirrel could never bring down an eagle. If the eagle wanted, he could swoop down and tear the squirrel to pieces with his powerful talons!"

"King Emmanuel is like that eagle," Sir Wisdom said quietly. "His power is limitless; his wisdom is eternal; his authority knows no bounds. Compared to the wisdom and power and majesty of Emmanuel, Argamor is but a squirrel with a pile of acorns. No matter how hard Argamor may try to knock the eagle down, it will soar forever! Emmanuel's throne is secure, my prince, and he will reign forever. Argamor and all his forces will be defeated before the battle is even joined."

"How do you know that, sire?"

"It is written within your book, Prince Josiah. Have you never read the last chapters? Your book tells the outcome of the final battle between Argamor and King Emmanuel. His Majesty will be victorious; Argamor will be defeated; and then Argamor and all who have followed him will be banished to a place of eternal torment. King Emmanuel and all who have followed him will reign forever. Nay, my prince, you need not fear that Argamor might be victorious, for your King has already won the victory!"

BOOK FOUR: THE TERRESTRIA CHRONICLES

Josiah reached out and handed the acorn back to his companion. "Then why does Argamor try? Does he not know that he will be defeated?"

"Argamor never gives up. He attempted to seize Emmanuel's throne once long ago," the old man replied with a chuckle, "and he failed miserably! He and his followers were banished from the Golden City. The history of Terrestria records countless other attempts by Argamor and his warriors, but every one of them have met with failure. This next and final attempt will be no different."

"Sire, what about the Crown of Kuros?" the young prince asked quietly. "What if Morphina delivers it to Argamor? If Argamor gained possession of the crown, would he not then rule Terrestria?"

"How much do you know about the Crown of Kuros?"

"Not much," Josiah admitted. "I had never even heard of it until two days ago when it was stolen."

"But what do you know?"

"Only what a knight at the table told me that night in the great hall. 'Kuros' is an ancient word meaning 'supremacy'. The Crown of Kuros is the symbol of King Emmanuel's supremacy over Terrestria; it is the token of his right to the throne. If Argamor should gain possession of the crown, he would then become the ruler of the entire kingdom." Prince Josiah looked at Sir Wisdom in alarm. "Sire, if that happens, Emmanuel would no longer be our King. Would we then owe allegiance to Argamor?"

Sir Wisdom gripped Josiah gently by the shoulders. "Who told you that the Crown of Kuros is the token of King Emmanuel's right to rule Terrestria?"

"One of the knights in the great hall of the Castle of Faith. I do not know his name, but he was seated at a table next to ours."

The old man shook his head. "He was mistaken, my prince. As I already explained, King Emmanuel is Lord of Terrestria forever. No one may claim his throne! Ever! The Crown of Kuros has nothing to do with the question of who will rule Terrestria, for that has already been decided forever."

"Then why is the Crown of Kuros so important, sire? What does it signify?"

Sir Wisdom turned and began to stroll back toward the campfire. "Possession of the Crown of Kuros," he said quietly, "determines who will reign in the heart of one person. If the crown is yielded to King Emmanuel, then His Majesty will reign within that heart. If the crown is given to another, that one then rules within the heart."

Josiah was confused. "The Crown of Kuros only signifies dominion over one heart? Whose heart is that?"

"The same one who allowed Morphina to steal the crown from the castle," the old man replied. "And since that person is the one who allowed the theft to take place, that person is the only one who can return the crown to its rightful place, under the control of King Emmanuel."

In an instant, the awful truth dawned upon the young prince. *I was the one who allowed the evil Morphina to steal the Crown of Kuros in the first place,* he told himself in dismay, *for in my selfishness, I was not careful to lock the treasure vault. And if I am the one who allowed her to take the crown, I am the only one who can get it back!*

Chapter Fifteen

Brilliant tongues of flame leaped high from the crackling campfire, creating mysterious shadows that danced on the trunks of the mighty oaks surrounding the clearing. Prince Josiah sat on a fallen log at the edge of the clearing, staring into the fire as though hypnotized by the bright figures that seemed to spring from the wood to leap and prance and disappear within the glowing caverns of the flames. Prince Selwyn and Sir Wisdom lay just beyond the fire, sound asleep in their bedrolls.

A glowing ember in the fire suddenly split apart with a loud snap, sending a shower of glowing sparks skyward like a thousand brilliant fireflies. Josiah stirred and looked up at the starry sky. The moon hung low in the heavens, a huge silver crescent against the deep black shroud of the night. The young prince sighed deeply. *I was the one who allowed the evil Morphina to steal the Crown of Kuros from the Castle of Faith,* he told himself with remorse, *and therefore, I am the only one who can recover it for King Emmanuel! But how do I find it? We have searched high and low for Morphina, but it seems that we see her only when she chooses to make an appearance.*

His heart smote him as he thought about the day that the evil enchantress had slipped into the castle and stolen the crown from the keep right under the very noses of the castle guards. "My lack of dedication to His Majesty enabled her to do it," he whispered aloud. "If my heart had been fully yielded to Emmanuel, this never would have happened!"

He thought about his visits to the future through the Lake of Destiny and groaned inwardly as he remembered the old hermit's journey to the Golden City to stand before King Emmanuel. "My life must not end in that manner!" he whispered fiercely. "My life *must* bring glory and honor to His Majesty. I must have gold, silver and precious jewels to offer my Lord when I stand before him. I want to hear him say, 'Well done'. My life must be yielded to my King, in order that I may honor him!"

He sighed again. "But how do I find the Crown of Kuros, in order that I may return it to His Majesty's treasure vault within the castle?"

"Prince Josiah," a gentle voice said softly, and the young prince jumped in fright.

He turned, and, to his astonishment, saw the ethereal white form of a lady standing at the edge of the forest. "Lady Prudence!" he exclaimed. "Wherefore are you come hither, my lady?" He rose and walked toward her.

"Josiah, my prince," the white lady replied softly, "I am sent hither with a message for you. The crown that you seek is presently in the possession of a fierce, fire-breathing dragon named Authades. You alone can defeat the great dragon, recover the Crown of Kuros for King Emmanuel, and restore the crown to its rightful place within the Castle of Faith. Prince Josiah, you must be the one to do battle with the dragon."

"The dragon breathes fire?" Josiah asked with a gulp.

Lady Prudence nodded. "Authades is indeed a very formidable adversary. You must not for one moment underestimate the dragon's cunning, strength, or determination to destroy you. Many a knight before you has been destroyed by this fierce beast. This will not be an easy quest, my prince, and you must go trusting completely in your King. Only as you surrender your heart to Emmanuel shall you be victorious and reclaim the crown for His Majesty."

"But I know not where to find the crown!" Josiah protested. "We have searched and searched, but have found no sign of the crown, or of Morphina, for that matter."

"You must go to the Forest of Decision," said the white lady softly. "There you will find silver parchments that will instruct you as to what you must do to find the Crown of Kuros. If your heart is surrendered, my prince, you shall be successful in your quest to recover the crown for His Majesty. But if your heart is still filled with selfishness and desire for personal glory, your quest will end in failure."

Prince Josiah frowned. "I cannot be sure of my own heart, my lady. It is deceitful above all things and desperately wicked; how can I know it? How will I know if my heart is surrendered to His Majesty, or if I am merely desiring vain glory for myself?"

"Why do you wish to find the Crown of Kuros?"

The question caught the young prince off guard. "I—I do not know," he stammered. "I want to return the crown to His Majesty's treasure vault, for that is the proper place for it. The Crown of Kuros rightly belongs to King Emmanuel, and yet, it is in the hands of another. I only wish to return the crown to King Emmanuel's control."

She studied him for a long moment without speaking. Josiah felt uncomfortable under her gaze; it was as though she could see into the very depths of his soul. Finally, she spoke. "Search your heart, my prince. For what reason?"

Josiah hesitated. "I—I want my heart to be yielded to my King," he whispered softly. "But I now know that my heart cannot be yielded until the Crown of Kuros is returned to His Majesty's treasure vault at the Castle of Faith. And that is why I simply must find the crown and bring it back to the castle."

The words seemed to spring of their own accord from his lips, but as he said them, he realized for the first time the truth of what he was saying. His heart was not fully surrendered to the will of Emmanuel. Surrender could only come when the Crown of Kuros was returned to the treasure vault at the Castle of Faith and he was the only one in the kingdom who could accomplish the return.

The white lady seemed pleased with his answer. "Well spoken, Prince Josiah. In reclaiming the Crown of Kuros for your King, you will yield your heart to him; and in yielding your heart, you reclaim the crown for him. It is true that one cannot take place without the other. Your words show that you are ready for this quest, my prince. Go tomorrow to the Forest of Decision. It is there that you will find the silver parchments that will direct you to the lair of Authades in order that you may slay the dragon and recover the Crown of Kuros for the honor of Emmanuel."

Fear and uncertainty sent a cold chill over Josiah's heart. "But I have never fought a dragon!" he protested. "How will I know what to do? Suppose that Authades prevails, and I lose the battle? Would that not dishonor the name of my King?"

Lady Prudence smiled, and Prince Josiah was dismayed to see that she was already starting to fade away.

"Wait, my lady," he begged. "Please tell me! What will happen to the honor of His Majesty if I lose the battle against Authades?"

"Go in faith, Prince Josiah," she replied, speaking so softly that the young prince could barely make out the words. She was fading rapidly, and Josiah could now see the forms of the trees behind her. "As you yield your heart to Emmanuel, you will prevail in the battle against Authades. And remember, you may send a petition to His Majesty at any time." With these words she was gone, vanishing like the mists before the morning sunshine.

Josiah returned to the campfire. He sat alone on the log and pondered the words of Lady Prudence. *As you yield your heart to Emmanuel, you will prevail in the battle against Authades. And remember, you may send a petition to His Majesty at any time.* He sighed. "King Emmanuel," he whispered, staring into the flames without seeing them, "I want so much for my heart to be yielded to you, but I find it so difficult! I want to stand before you one day and hear you say 'Well done' and know that I have honored your name. I want to present gold, silver, and precious stones to you, and know that my life has accomplished that which pleases you. But I find it so hard to yield my heart!"

He stood to his feet. *I will leave at first light,* he decided. *I will make my way to the Forest of Decision, find the silver parchments and follow their directions to the lair of Authades, slay the dragon, and recover the Crown of Kuros for King Emmanuel.* His heart pounded with anticipation as he crawled into his bedroll and fell fast asleep.

The morning was dark, cold, and misty as the young prince awoke and crept quietly from his bedroll. The sun was not yet up but a faint pink glow was just beginning to brighten the eastern sky. Daylight was not far behind. Josiah rubbed his eyes and surveyed the campsite. Wispy fingers of fog swirled across the hillside, moving and changing shape like the hands of a living creature. Sir Wisdom and Selwyn lay quietly sleeping. The ashes of the fire, now dead, still managed to send forth an occasional wisp of smoke.

Josiah crept down to a little stream that trickled down the hillside. Kneeling in the carpet of leaves, he dipped up a double handful of water and washed his face. He dipped up another handful and drank deeply. His heart beat faster as he thought about the perilous quest that he was about to commence.

How will I prevail against Authades? I've never even seen a dragon, much less done battle with one! What if I am defeated? What if Authades kills me? Will the thing become known across Terrestria, and will His Majesty's name be dishonored?

Opening his book and taking the parchment from within its pages, Prince Josiah prepared to send a petition to Emmanuel. He quickly wrote the following message:

"Your Majesty,

Even if I die in the attempt, I will return the Crown of Kuros to the keep at the Castle of Faith. My lord, I want you to have my heart, and I know that my heart will never be yielded to you until the crown is returned to the keep. I am told that I must face a fierce dragon to recover the crown, and I humbly ask for your help. I cannot complete this quest alone.

For the honor of your majestic name,

Your son, Prince Josiah."

Josiah rolled the parchment tightly, opened his fingers, and watched as the petition disappeared over the looming crest of the mountain. The message had scarcely left his hand when he turned and headed up the hill, walking quietly through the fallen leaves so as not to disturb Selwyn and Sir Wisdom.

He had walked about a furlong when he heard a rustling in the undergrowth. Turning, he was surprised to see Lady Prudence step from the shadows. "Josiah, my prince," she called softly.

"My lady," the young prince replied, somewhat taken back at the suddenness of the white lady's appearance. "I did not expect to see you this morning."

"I have come to wish you success in your quest to destroy the dragon," the lady said softly, with a trace of a smile playing at the corners of her mouth. "You are determined, and that is good. You will no doubt be successful in your quest. The Crown of Kuros will be safe once it is within your hands."

"I am grateful for your confidence in me," Josiah replied humbly. Deep inside, he was not so sure that he would be able to face the dragon. He was trusting in his King, and yet, there was some doubt.

It was as though Lady Prudence could read his thoughts. "You will do just fine," she assured him. "In no time at all the dragon will be dispatched, you will be victorious, and the Crown of Kuros will be on its way back to the Castle of Faith. That is what you still desire, is it not?"

Josiah nodded earnestly. "Of course, my lady." He gave a nervous laugh. "I'm just not sure that it will be that easy. I'm just grateful that I have the sword that King Emmanuel gave me."

She gave him a strange look. "You didn't leave your sword at the campsite?"

Josiah was puzzled by her words. "Leave my sword, my lady? Why would I leave my sword behind?"

A strange smile crossed her exquisite features. "I forgot that this is your first time to fight a dragon. You must face Authades without your sword, my prince. Were you to take it into the dragon's lair, the victory would not really be yours, and that would be a rather hollow victory. Remember what I told you last night? 'You alone can defeat the dragon, recover the crown for King Emmanuel, and restore it to its rightful place within the Castle of Faith.' Alone, Prince Josiah. You must not take even your sword. You must face Authades alone."

Josiah trembled at the idea. "I must take my sword, my lady! It is my only assurance of victory."

But the white lady shook her head. "Nay, my prince. This is the only way. You must go alone, without your sword. Leave it at the campsite before you attempt to find the dragon's lair." Without another word, Lady Prudence faded from view.

Stunned by the words of the ethereal visitor, the young prince stood staring at the spot where she had appeared just moments before. *How can I possibly slay a dragon without my sword?* he thought desperately. *I have no strength of my own.*

Determined nevertheless to follow the instructions he had received, Josiah retraced his steps to the campsite. Creeping silently through the carpet of leaves so as not to waken Selwyn or Sir Wisdom, he carefully placed the book inside his bed-roll, though his heart seemed to tell him that it was mistake to leave his only weapon behind. *If I am to fight a fierce, fire-breathing dragon, should I not use my sword?* he asked himself. *How can I hope to have victory if I go unarmed against a foe that is mightier than I? I will surely be killed, and my defeat will bring no honor to King Emmanuel. And then who is to return the Crown of Kuros to its proper place within the Castle of Faith?*

Bewildered by the white lady's insistence that he leave his sword behind, Josiah took one last look at the invincible weapon and then turned away. He sensed that the battle with the dragon Authades would be the fiercest conflict that he had yet faced, and yet, somehow, he was to win the victory without a weapon. He shook his head. It just didn't make sense. An uneasy feeling of impending doom swept over him as he trudged fearfully up the hill.

Chapter Sixteen

Prince Josiah found the trail to the Forest of Decision with
no trouble at all. He hiked quickly down the narrow path,
determined to locate the silver parchments, discover Authades'
lair, and do battle with the dragon in order to recover the
Crown of Kuros. In truth, he was dreading the encounter with
the dragon, and he simply wanted to get it over as quickly as
possible.

"I still do not understand," he said aloud. "Why would Lady
Prudence insist that I leave my sword back at Sir Wisdom's
camp? If I am to face a fire-breathing dragon, I will need my
sword like never before! I cannot hope to win the battle against
Authades unless I am armed with the invincible weapon given
me by King Emmanuel."

The path wound its way down through a narrow, wooded glen
bounded on both sides by steep slopes covered with thorn trees
and brambles. The ground was soggy, oozing brackish water at
Josiah's every step. The air became cold and chill, and the young
prince gathered his cloak more tightly about him. To the east,
the sky was brightening rapidly but darkness hovered over the
glen, causing Josiah's feelings of trepidation to increase. *If I had
my sword,* he told himself ruefully, *I would also have a light to guide*

me through this dark valley. He shivered and pressed forward, determined not to fail in his quest to recover the crown for Emmanuel.

As he reached the far side of the glen he began to make his way through clusters of large plants with broad, waxy leaves that hugged the ground. He struggled to push his way through. Slowly realizing that he was hearing numerous tiny voices, he paused to listen. The voices stopped immediately.

After a moment of silence, the young prince started forward and again heard the mysterious voices. It was as if scores of invisible people were following him, even surrounding him. Once again, he stopped abruptly and the strange voices ceased just as abruptly. He frowned as he tried to figure out the puzzling situation.

He took two slow, deliberate steps and then stopped. Again, the bizarre voices were plainly audible when he moved but hushed instantly when he stopped. He caught his breath. The voices were coming from beneath the leafy plants!

Prince Josiah stood completely still for several long moments, holding his breath, listening intently, and watching the unusual plants very closely. And then, out of the corner of his eye, he saw the barest trace of movement. A tiny human figure had peeked from beneath one of the leaves and then darted back again!

Josiah pounced, leaping toward the spot and thrusting the leaf to one side in one quick movement. A tiny man less than ten inches tall scrambled for cover but the young prince seized him in one hand and snatched him from the ground before he could make his escape. "Release me!" the tiny figure bellowed, struggling and kicking with all his might.

"A Littlekin!" Josiah gasped in astonishment. "Why are you following me? How many of you are there?"

At that moment, the woods came alive as hordes of the tiny folk appeared from beneath the foliage. Josiah's mind flashed back to the encounter he had had with the Littlekins on his quest for the seven castles. The tiny folk had captured and bound him and then taken him back to their village for trial before an unreasonable magistrate. The young prince had escaped only by using Emmanuel's sword.

Josiah panicked. *I don't have my sword!* Dropping the furious Littlekin, he whirled about and dashed from the glen. The sounds of the angry mob of pursuing Littlekins prompted him to run for his life.

On the far side of the ridge Josiah slowed and glanced behind him. There was no sign of pursuit; he had outrun the Littlekins. He hurried down the path and entered the campsite to find Selwyn and Sir Wisdom sitting before a cheerful fire. They both looked up as he approached. "Your quest has caused you to rise early, Prince Josiah," the nobleman observed.

"Sire, I have found the Crown of Kuros!" Josiah blurted eagerly.

"Found the crown, have you?" Sir Wisdom replied. "And where did you find it, pray tell?"

"Well, sire, I haven't exactly found it yet," the young prince hastily corrected himself, "but I know how to find it. Lady Prudence told me. I'm to go to the Forest of Decision where I will find silver parchments that will give me directions to the lair of a terrible, fire-breathing dragon. If I can defeat the dragon, I will recover the crown for King Emmanuel."

"I'll go with you," Selwyn offered, but Sir Wisdom laid a hand on his arm.

"This is one quest on which you cannot accompany your friend." The old man turned to Josiah. "So you're off to do battle with Authades, are you?"

Josiah stared at him. "How did you know about the dragon?"

"Authades is a terrible adversary," Sir Wisdom replied, ignoring Josiah's question. "In the ancient language, his name means 'self-pleasing' or 'self-willed'. He has wounded many a knight of King Emmanuel and destroyed the life and reputation of many others. Anyone who would fight this dragon must not for one moment underestimate the beast's cunning, strength, or determination to destroy. To enter the lair of Authades and do battle with the dragon is to take one's life in one's hands."

He gave Josiah a searching look. "So why do you, my prince, presume to do battle with this monster unarmed? The sword of Emmanuel is the only way one could ever hope to defeat Authades, and yet you have left your sword here at camp."

Josiah stepped to the fire and warmed his hands. "I wanted to take my sword, sire, for I feel helpless as a newborn babe without it, but Lady Prudence insisted that I must leave it behind when I go to fight Authades. Just now I am returning to camp to retrieve the sword because I have encountered some Littlekins."

"Little Sins?" Sir Wisdom prompted.

"Aye," Josiah replied. "There were scores of them, perhaps hundreds."

At the moment, Sir Wisdom wasn't concerned with the little people. "My sister instructed you to fight Authades without your sword? Lad, that's preposterous! Lady Prudence knows that you can never hope to defeat the dragon in your own strength. You simply must use the sword given to you by King Emmanuel! There is no other way."

"Lady Prudence *did* tell me not to take the sword into the battle, sire," Josiah protested, "though I could not understand why. I tried to reason with her, but she insisted that the sword must be left behind."

The old man shook his head. "Lad, that doesn't make sense! Lady Prudence would never tell you that, for she would be setting you up for a certain defeat. There is not a knight in the entire kingdom of Terrestria that could hope to go unarmed against the dragon."

"But she did tell me that, sire!" Josiah insisted. "She met me by the way this morning and demanded that I take my sword back to your campsite. I obeyed, and I have hidden it in my bedroll."

Sir Wisdom was thoughtful. "You say that a lady met you on the path and told you not to take your sword?"

Josiah nodded. "It was Lady Prudence, sire."

The nobleman shook his head. "It was not Lady Prudence that appeared to you, Prince Josiah. My sister would never tell you—"

"Morphina!" Selwyn guessed. "Josiah, it was Morphina, posing as Lady Prudence!"

Without a word, Josiah turned and looked at Sir Wisdom.

The old man nodded. "He's right, lad. The woman you saw was the enchantress, not my sister. Morphina was contriving to lay a trap for you! Had you gone unarmed to the lair of

Authades, you would have been defeated for certain. You could have been maimed or killed."

Josiah was angry. "Morphina again! How can we be rid of that evil woman?"

"Perhaps we never shall in this life," Sir Wisdom replied quietly. "I expect that we shall be plagued by her treacherous ways until His Majesty returns from the Golden City."

He squatted before the fire and stirred the contents of a small pot that hung over the flames, bubbling and hissing and sending forth a delicious aroma that suddenly made Josiah's mouth water. "Have some breakfast, my prince, and then you shall resolve your quest for the Crown of Kuros this very day. Prince Selwyn will make his way back to the Castle of Faith, but if you wish, I shall accompany you to the dragon's lair."

Prince Josiah slowed as he and Sir Wisdom approached the dense thicket of brambles in the darkness of the forbidding glen. "This is as far as I came, sire. The Littlekins were hiding under the plants just beyond." He drew the book from his doublet, changed it into his sword, and started forward.

"Charge!" cried a tiny voice. A vast horde of Littlekin soldiers exploded from beneath the waxy leaves and swarmed toward Josiah. Smartly dressed in red doublets with gold braid, white leggings, and shiny black boots, the tiny warriors carried swords, lances and cross-bows. Numbering in the hundreds, they were led by a stern-faced officer by the name of Captain Temptation.

Prince Josiah swung his mighty sword, scattering the tiny

troops left and right. *I have them now,* he thought, with a note of vicious triumph.

Screaming with rage, scores of unnoticed Littlekin warriors abruptly dropped from the branches of the trees overhead to land upon Josiah's back and shoulders. Tiny as they were, their combined weight was too much for the young prince. He stumbled and fell to the ground.

"Sir Wisdom," he cried in desperation, "help me! These wretched Littlekins will be the death of me!"

"I am here for you, my prince," came the nobleman's reply from a distance, "but this is a battle that you must face alone."

Josiah fought bravely, throwing his arms wide and hurling his tiny tormentors in all directions. He tried to rise to his feet but hordes of other little soldiers leaped upon him as fast as he could throw the first ones off. There were so many Littlekins clinging to his sword arm and shoulder that he could not even wield the weapon.

"I am weary and my strength is gone," Josiah cried out at last. "I cannot fight any longer!"

"Fight in the strength of your King," Sir Wisdom called. "His strength is your strength, and only in his strength can you prevail."

"Your Majesty," the young prince cried, summoning all his strength to hold his sword aloft with trembling hands, "I can no longer fight in my own strength! I must have your strength, or I am vanquished before I even reach Authades' lair. It is for your honor and glory, my King, that I have set upon this quest! It is for the honor of your name, my Lord, that I seek to return the Crown of Kuros to the keep of the Castle of Faith."

At that moment his attention was arrested by the raucous cries of numerous birds. Enormous blackbirds by the hundreds came swooping into the glen and began to snatch the Littlekins in their claws. With shrill cries of terror the tiny soldiers abandoned their assault on the young prince and dashed for the safety of the waxy-leafed plants.

Prince Josiah leaped to his feet and dashed up the slope. In a moment he had left the glen and the Littlekins behind and hurried upward along a winding path through the forest. He looked around. Sir Wisdom was not in sight. He opened his mouth to call out, but for some unexplained reason refrained from doing so.

A golden beam of sunlight splashed across the trail, lifting his spirits and helping him to forget the horrors of the encounter with the Littlekins. He would continue on with the quest. He would find the silver parchments, locate and slay the great dragon Authades, and recover the Crown of Kuros for King Emmanuel. Once the crown was returned to the keep where it belonged, his heart would be yielded to Emmanuel. He found that he could hardly wait. His heart cried out for surrender to the will of his King.

At that moment he heard a cry of pain. He stopped at the sound, listening intently and hardly daring to breathe. The cry came again, a low moan of anguish that sent a shiver of uneasiness through Josiah's soul. He sighed. Someone was in need of assistance. He would stop and help, but his heart was impatient to continue the quest for the crown.

Josiah gasped as a knight came stumbling down the trail, bleeding profusely from numerous wounds. His armor was battered and dented and blackened as if it had been through a fire. Part of it was torn away, exposing one arm, which was blistered and badly burned. The knight had no sword or lance and his visor was down, concealing his face. As the young prince watched in stunned silence, the warrior stumbled, reached out one gauntleted hand as if to ask for help, and then fell to the earth with a loud crash.

Prince Josiah hesitated for just an instant and then sprang to the side of the badly injured knight. Dropping to his knees beside the pathetic form, he asked, "What can I do for you, sire? Tell me how I may be of help."

The knight lay still, and for just an instant, Josiah feared that he was dead.

The man's right hand twitched and then slowly rose until it was touching the battered helmet. The knight was attempting to raise his visor. Grasping the man's visor with both hands, Josiah raised it for him. He saw a bloody, blackened face that was contorted with pain. "Thank you, my lord," a strained voice said. "I am grateful."

"Can—can I get you some water, sire?" Josiah croaked, overcome at the sight of the man's injuries. "I passed a stream just a moment ago."

The helmet moved slightly, and the young prince realized that the knight was trying to nod his head. "I would—" The feeble voice faltered. The wounded knight tried again. "I would be grateful."

Josiah leaped to his feet and ran toward the stream. Lacking a vessel in which to carry water, he removed his cloak and immersed it in the clear, shallow water. Cupping his hands beneath the sodden garment, he dashed back to the side of the stricken knight. He knelt and allowed water to trickle into the man's mouth. The knight drank gratefully.

"I am indebted to you, my lord," the warrior gasped when he had finished drinking. He dropped his head back to the ground and closed his eyes, breathing deeply.

"What happened, sire?" the young prince asked as he prepared to clean the bleeding wounds and salve the horrible burns. "How is it that you are so sorely wounded?"

"I have fought the most fearsome beast that ever existed," the knight replied in a weak voice that trembled with exhaustion. "I have faced the terror of Terrestria and barely escaped with my life! What a fool I was to think that I could hope to conquer such a terrible monster! I have come within an inch of death!"

Josiah gulped and swallowed hard. "What is this beast of which you speak, sire?"

The knight groaned. His eyes closed and a tremor played throughout his body, starting at his head and coursing down to his feet. Gritting his teeth and inhaling deeply as if to gather his strength, the wounded man opened his eyes and turned his head toward Prince Josiah. "The monster of which I speak, my lord, is the great dragon Authades."

Chapter Seventeen

Prince Josiah caught his breath at the mention of the dragon's name. A cold knot of fear tightened in his stomach. His heart pounded fiercely. The wounded knight had faced the very same dragon that the young prince had hoped to conquer, but the poor man had barely managed to escape with his life. His wounds and burns were very serious, perhaps the worst that Josiah had ever seen, and he wondered if the man would even survive. If he dared to go against the dragon, perhaps he would meet with the same horrible fate. He trembled as he thought about it.

This poor knight is broad of shoulder and half a foot taller than I am, he told himself as he prepared to tend to the man's terrible wounds. *He is a stalwart knight if ever I saw one. Since he fared this badly against Authades, how can I possibly hope to fare any better?*

The injured knight groaned aloud as the young prince began to wash his wounds. Josiah took a deep breath. "Tell me about the dragon Authades," he said softly. "What happened? How went the battle?" Perhaps the misfortunate knight could provide some bit of useful information; and at any rate, the telling of his experience would serve to take the man's mind off his pain and injuries.

"Authades cannot be described, my lord," the knight whispered through clenched teeth. "Words fail me to tell of the terrors I experienced as I came face to face with this fearsome beast! His scales are like armor; his teeth are like swords; and his breath is like the blast of a fiery furnace. My heart nearly failed me as I attempted to do battle with the raging monster. His strength is incredible; his cunning past finding out; his rage is overwhelming." The knight shuddered. "Nay, my lord, I cannot describe Authades for you."

Josiah tore a strip from his own doublet to serve as a bandage. He began to remove a section of the man's armor to reach the worst of the wounds. "But won't you try, sire?" he pleaded. "How big is the dragon? Does he have armored scales? Did you observe any weak areas where the dragon might be vulnerable to attack?"

The knight gritted his teeth and turned to look the young prince squarely in the eye. "Your questions, my lord, tell me that you are thinking of making an assault on the dragon. Surely you would not consider such a foolhardy undertaking?"

Prince Josiah swallowed hard. He hesitated. "Sire, I am presently on my way to fight Authades."

The knight's eyes grew wide and he raised his head and shoulders, grunting with the effort. "Nay, my lord! You must not even think of such a thing. You are but a youth. Authades would kill you in an instant!"

"I must go, sire," Josiah said firmly. "The matter is already decided; my mind is already made up. I must fight Authades."

"Lad, you do not know what you are saying," the knight protested. "The dragon is huge—bigger than a house! His body is covered with armored scales that can turn the sharpest arrows and blunt the strongest spears. He snorts fire like blasts from a furnace! Should you arouse his anger, he would slay you in an instant!"

"Nevertheless I will go," Josiah said resolutely. "I must recover the Crown of Kuros for the honor of His Majesty, King Emmanuel. My mind is made up and there is no turning back."

"Oh, if only you knew what you are saying," the knight lamented, clutching the sides of his helmet with his steel-shrouded hands. "You are no match for the likes of Authades, my lord. You may be a strong warrior, skilled in the use of the sword and the bow, but you would not even know how to begin to fight against the great dragon. No weapon ever devised has been successful against him. He can change his form at will, even render himself invisible when he chooses. How could you hope to fight against a monster such as that?"

Prince Josiah's faith was beginning to waver. "I shall go in the strength and power of King Emmanuel," he declared, though the knight's dire warnings were already causing him to have second thoughts. "I shall use the mighty sword that he has given me. I shall claim the victory over Authades in the name of His Majesty."

The knight laughed, grimacing in pain as he did. "They will bury you in the name of His Majesty," he retorted, "if there is anything left of you to bury! Authades will burn you alive. He will roast you like a pig on a spit."

He clutched Josiah's hand, the steel of his gauntlet squeezing the boy's flesh until Josiah winced in pain. "My lord, listen to me," the knight pleaded. "Look at me! Can you not see what that bloodthirsty dragon has done to me? I fought hard, my lord, fought with all my heart and soul, but it was no use! I simply was no match for the power of the dragon, and I assure you, it will be no different with you. Authades snorts blasts of flame fifty feet long, lad! If you go against him, your armor and shield will provide no protection. He will kill you in an instant."

The wounded knight continued to plead with the young prince as Josiah removed sections of his armor and bandaged his wounds. He did his best to talk Josiah out of his plans to do battle with the dragon, but the young prince was determined not to be dissuaded. Prince Josiah argued with the man, pointing out that he was going in the strength of Emmanuel, that he had the sword designed by His Majesty himself, and that victory had already been promised. He mentioned his desire to see the Crown of Kuros returned to the keep at the Castle of Faith in order that his own heart might be fully surrendered to the will of the King. The knight continued to reason with him, doing his best to build fear within the heart of the valiant young prince.

"It's no use!" the knight finally declared, throwing up his hands in despair as Josiah finished the bandaging. "You are determined to march needlessly to your death, are you not, my lord?"

"I am not marching to my death," the young prince countered, though he was beginning to entertain some doubts. "I am marching to the den of Authades to defeat the dragon once and for all in order that the Crown of Kuros may be returned to the keep at the castle where it belongs! I fight in the name of my King, Emmanuel, and I claim victory in his name. Talk no more of my death, wretched knight, for your words of fear cannot cause me to turn back. My heart is fixed on this one objective— I will fight the dragon!"

The knight gave a long, mournful sigh. "Very well, my lord.

Now, would you be so kind as to help me back into my armor?"

Josiah worked quickly, helping the injured knight dress out in his armor once more. Neither said a word until the last pieces, the greaves upon the knight's shins, were strapped into place. To the surprise of the young prince, the knight immediately stood to his feet. "So my pleas cannot turn you from your intent to do battle with Authades, can they? Then my sword shall!"

The knight's voice was strong and steady, in bold contrast with the feeble voice of earlier moments. It was a voice that was quite familiar. The young prince spun around in astonishment. "Palaios! Palaios Anthropos!"

Palaios stood tall, sword in hand, ready to do battle. "You will never face the dragon, my young prince, for there is too much at stake if you should be victorious and return the Crown of Kuros to King Emmanuel. The crown must stay where it is; I cannot afford for you to recover it. Your success would ruin everything for which I have worked so hard." He lowered the sword until the blade was pointed at Josiah's heart, menacing and deadly. "Prince Josiah, I must warn you—if you take one step toward the Forest of Decision, I will run you through!"

The young prince took several quick steps backwards, but only so that he might draw his own sword. Swinging the mighty weapon with both hands, Josiah shouted, "You shall not hinder me, Palaios Anthropos, you treacherous blackguard! I will not be in bondage to my old nature. The crown shall be returned to King Emmanuel."

"Then prepare to die," Palaios retorted, "for one of us will not leave this wood alive." With these words, he leaped forward, swinging his broadsword with both hands in a sudden move that was intended to take off the head of the young prince.

Josiah was prepared and met steel with steel. Swinging the sword of Emmanuel with all his strength, he countered the knight's vicious attack, dealing blow for blow. He soon found that Palaios was a determined foe and did not give up easily. Swords clashed, and the forest rang with the sounds of the desperate conflict.

"Surrender your sword," the tall knight demanded, grunting with the effort of wielding his own weapon, as he took a particularly vicious swing at Josiah. "You will accomplish nothing by resisting! If you persist in this foolish quest to locate the lair of Authades, I shall be forced to slay you on the spot."

"I will surrender this sword to no one but His Majesty," the young prince retorted, parrying the slashes and thrusts of the knight's broadsword, "and no one shall stop me from finding and slaying the dragon. The Crown of Kuros must be returned to the Castle of Faith!"

"You are a stout-hearted lad, and I admire your determination, but are you willing to forfeit your life to recover the crown?" The knight's sword slashed through the air. "I warn you again, Prince Josiah, if you do not turn back at once, I shall drop you right here and now!"

Josiah didn't answer. Gripping his mighty sword with both hands and swinging with every bit of energy that he possessed, he fought desperately. The ferocity of his countermoves and the skill of his swordsmanship took his adversary by surprise. Within moments, he found that he was driving Palaios backwards. No longer on the defensive, he cornered the tall knight against an outcropping of granite.

Palaios fought back viciously, desperately, but the young prince had gained the upper hand. Josiah's sword pierced the tall knight's armor, inflicting a mortal wound. Moments later, Palaios Anthropos lay dead upon the ground. The young prince felt an inner sadness akin to pain as he surveyed the body lying in the grass. Though his tall adversary had caused him grief on several occasions, for some unexplainable reason he felt almost as if a part of himself had just died.

"Well done, Prince Josiah!"

Josiah turned at the salutation to see Sir Wisdom hurrying up the trail toward him. "Sir Wisdom! Sire, I thought you had deserted me."

"I would not desert you, Prince Josiah. I simply had to make myself scarce so that this wicked Palaios would make his appearance. It is far better for you to have faced him here and now, than for you to have to contend with him at the same time that you are battling Authades."

The young prince nodded to show that he understood. "Will you accompany me to the Forest of Decision to find the silver parchments?"

"I shall accompany you all the way, my prince," the old nobleman answered quietly. "I plan to witness your battle against Authades, and perchance even assist if I am needed."

"Then let us make haste," Josiah suggested. "I am anxious to engage the dragon and win the Crown of Kuros for His Majesty."

The old man and the youth hurried up the trail toward the Forest of Decision. In his eagerness to recover the crown, Josiah traveled at a gait that could almost be called a run, striding along so quickly that Sir Wisdom struggled to keep pace. But the old man never complained or called for a rest.

Recognizing the zeal for the crown that motivated the young prince, he was determined not to hinder the quest in any way.

After several furlongs of travel, the man and the youth descended a gentle slope and found themselves approaching an obscure village at the base of a precipitous mountain. Josiah studied the hamlet as they approached, feeling that there was something vaguely familiar about the place, though he could not identify it. It was only when he saw the crumbling, half-finished wall and filthy, decaying buildings that he recognized the town. "The Village of Indifference," he said in disgust. "Such a wretched, dismal place. How thankful I am that I do not live here!"

"The residents of this miserable village have come here by choice, my prince," Sir Wisdom replied.

Josiah nodded. "I know, sire. Many times I have sent petitions to His Majesty, asking that he would enable me to guard my heart against indifference, that I may never come here."

The roar of a crowd caught the attention of the two travelers, and they looked down over an embankment to see scores of townspeople gathered along the banks of a narrow, muddy watercourse. Several men were standing in the stream, preparing to release tiny boats made of reeds. "Another sailing," the young prince remarked in disdain. "The walls of their village are falling down and their houses are desperately in need of repair, and yet they spend their days building and sailing those worthless little boats! If only they could see how fulfilling, how satisfying, is a life of service to Emmanuel."

Sir Wisdom nodded in agreement without answering.

Leaving the contemptible village behind, they continued on toward the Forest of Decision in order to find the silver parchments of which Lady Prudence had spoken. The path led across some rugged terrain but the old man and the prince pressed resolutely onward. After a time, they entered a dark, shadowy wood. "The Forest of Decision," Prince Josiah said aloud. "Perchance we are almost there."

A short while later they came upon a clearing nestled between two mountain ridges. At the north end, a mountain stream thundered over a thirty-foot precipice to cascade into a shallow, rocky pool and then flow merrily across a grassy meadow bright with wildflowers. Directly across from the waterfall, three huge oaks stood shoulder to shoulder, tall and stately, as if they were guarding the secluded dell. In the very center of the clearing stood an immense table-like formation of the purest white stone, and upon the formation, a huge silver scroll that glistened and shimmered with all the colors of the rainbow. The handles of the massive volume were adorned with precious stones of all varieties and colors.

"The silver parchments," Josiah said softly, quite awed by the spectacle, "just like Lady Prudence said."

Chapter Eighteen

Glancing at Sir Wisdom for reassurance, the young prince cautiously entered the clearing. His heart pounded as he approached the huge, glowing scroll resting on the rocky pedestal. The ornate volume was closed, and, to his surprise, was secured by a large silver clasp with an oblong keyhole. He turned to Sir Wisdom. "How do I open it, sire? I have no key."

"Use the Key of Faith from your book, my prince," the old man replied quietly. He stood at the edge of the clearing, ten or fifteen paces from the rock formation and the silver scroll.

Josiah drew his book from his clothing, opened it, and took out a tiny golden key. With a trembling hand he inserted the key into the hole of the silver clasp. He jumped in surprise as the clasp sprang open with a sharp click that echoed across the secluded glen. As he watched in fascinated silence, the handles of the massive scroll parted slowly, as if moved by an unseen hand. A brilliant aura of pure white light radiated from the volume, blinding in its intensity. The scroll began to unroll, and the awed young prince could see that the parchment was filled with an exquisite flowing script. The scroll opened to a predetermined page somewhere near the center of the volume. The brilliant light diminished slightly, so Josiah felt that it was safe to draw closer.

Returning his book to its place within his doublet, the young prince paused reverently before the giant silver scroll. The selected page contained a terse message. "Sow the seed from your book," he read aloud.

Perplexed by the instructions, he turned and crept back to Sir Wisdom. "What seed is it referring to, sire?"

"Open your book and find out," the old man suggested with a hint of amusement playing across his features.

Josiah complied, drawing the book from his raiment and opening the cover. As he did, a large quantity of golden grain cascaded from within to pour upon the slab of rock at his feet. He stooped and ran his hands through the seed. "Where should I plant this, sire?"

The look of amusement returned to Sir Wisdom's face. "Perhaps right here in the clearing, my prince."

Prince Josiah scooped up two handfuls of the seed grain and stood to his feet. With a brisk, side-handed motion, he began to scatter the seed far and wide. The grain sparkled like gold dust as it flew through the air to land upon the ground. When his hands were empty, he stood back and watched.

Loud, raucous cries drew Josiah's attention heavenward and he looked up in dismay as a flock of large, noisy blackbirds descended upon the clearing and began eagerly to consume the seed grain that he had just sowed. Angered, the young prince started to leap forward to chase away the birds, but Sir Wisdom touched his shoulder, holding him back. "It is too late to change the results, my prince," the nobleman said quietly. "Just observe what happens."

The flock of birds pecked away furiously at the ground, crying and fighting and squawking until every last seed had been devoured. When the grain was gone, they lifted their wings and took to the air, screeching hideously. The old man and the boy watched in silence until the flock disappeared over the treetops.

"They have devoured every last seed, sire," Josiah lamented. "Why did you not allow me to drive them away?"

"You have sowed seed by the wayside," Sir Wisdom replied. "The ground is hard and infertile. Even if the birds had not devoured it, the seed would have produced nothing there."

"Perhaps I should try again," the young prince suggested. "Perhaps if I sow the seed in another location?"

The old man nodded without speaking.

Prince Josiah gathered another double handful of the precious seed and walked across the clearing. He scattered the kernels of grain across a rocky, moss-covered slope that was adorned by an occasional wildflower. When the task was completed, he stepped back to watch. Sir Wisdom joined him.

To Josiah's surprise, tiny green shoots sprang up almost immediately. He was delighted as he watched the tender plants grow faster and faster, each one reaching upward as if determined to outdo its neighbors. Within moments, the new plants were nearly two feet tall.

Josiah turned to Sir Wisdom. "These are doing better than the last ones." But even as he spoke, the seedlings abruptly stopped growing, trembled for a moment as if stricken with the palsy, and then began to droop. Within moments, every last one had withered and died.

"Sire, I do not understand it. These were doing so well."

"There was no depth of earth here, my prince. These plants had no root, and so were scorched by the sun, withered, and died. Why not try again?"

With a sigh, Josiah returned to the small pile of golden seed, dipped up two handfuls, and chose another spot. With energetic sweeping motions he spread the seed far and wide. Sir Wisdom appeared at his elbow as he stepped back to await the results.

Just as before, tiny green shoots appeared almost instantly. As the young prince watched anxiously, the tender green plants began to grow, slowly at first and then faster and faster until they were eagerly climbing skyward. Josiah let out a sigh of relief. "These will do better," he told Sir Wisdom. "The soil is deeper here, and the plants will have good roots."

But even as he spoke a number of dark-colored plants sprang up from the earth and began to grow among the tender green plants. The new plants were woody and thorny and soon outgrew the tender green wheat. As Josiah watched in dismay, the thorns began to wrap their stalks around the stems of the wheat, choking and smothering the plants until they had all withered and died.

"It's no use, sire," the young prince told Sir Wisdom, expressing his disappointment in a long sigh. "The seed just will not do well here."

"There is nothing wrong with the seed," the old man told him. "The trouble is with the ground upon which you have planted." He smiled. "What you have just seen is a picture of the human heart."

Josiah was confused. "What do you mean, sire?"

"The seed that you are sowing is the word of King Emmanuel," Sir Wisdom explained. "The hard ground represents the hardness of a human heart. Those who hear it but do not understand it do not properly receive it. Just as the blackbirds did, Argamor comes and snatches away the King's words with doubt, confusion and unbelief.

"You saw the seed on the stony ground spring up almost immediately, and then wither and die. There are those in the kingdom who have received Emmanuel's words with gladness, but have no depth of conviction and no root of faith in His Majesty. In times of persecution or trouble they wither away.

"The seed on the thorny ground also grew quickly, but you saw what took place. The thorns choked the plants and killed them. Some within the kingdom of Terrestria receive the word for awhile, but then are choked out by the cares of this world and the deceitfulness of riches. They too are as worthless as the first two and bring forth no fruit worthy of His Majesty."

"But will the grain not grow here?" Josiah asked. "Thus far, all of my sowing has produced nothing!"

"Try over there, in that fertile soil by the stream," the old nobleman suggested. "I think you will be pleased with the results."

With a shrug of his shoulders, the young prince gathered another double handful of grain and walked toward the stream. Hardly daring to hope for better results, he began to scatter the seed over the dark loam along the banks of the little brook. When his hands were empty, he stepped back to await the outcome. After several minutes, nothing had happened, and he turned to Sir Wisdom in disappointment and disgust. "Sire, this was no better. I see nothing!"

The old man smiled. "Have patience, my prince. This will take a little longer."

When Josiah turned back to the plot of ground by the stream he was gratified to see small green shoots pushing their way through the soil. As he watched, they grew taller and taller, some not as fast as others, but all growing steadily. His delight grew as the plants became straight and sturdy—tall, healthy plants that he knew would survive and produce. Within moments, heads of grain appeared on each stalk, ripening gradually until they were a beautiful golden color.

"Behold, sire," the young prince cried in delight, "this good ground has produced a bountiful harvest of grain!"

"Aye, a picture of a good heart open to Emmanuel's words. This is the heart that produces a harvest honoring to His Majesty. My prince, always guard your heart for His Majesty that it might always be receptive to his words and produce that which is worthy of Emmanuel's name."

"Sire, what shall I do now? I still must find the lair of that vile beast, Authades."

The old man pointed to the silver scroll. "Follow the instructions upon the page of the parchment."

Josiah stepped close to the rocky projection and gazed at the open page of the huge silver scroll. "To receive protection from the vapors," he read aloud, "harvest the grain and eat thereof." He turned to Sir Wisdom. "Of what vapors does it speak, sire?"

"The den of Authades is known to be corrupted with vapors that are injurious and downright deadly to the human heart. Were you to enter the dragon's lair without protection, you could be overcome be the poisonous vapors."

"But how will eating the grain protect me?" Josiah wondered.

"Do you not realize what the harvest of grain is?"

The young prince shook his head.

"The grain from the harvest is the result of an obedient heart that has heeded the words of King Emmanuel. It is the result of applying His Majesty's commands to the heart and life. A heart that is thus prepared to do Emmanuel's will is protected against the deadly vapors within the dragon's cavern."

Prince Josiah stepped forward and gathered a handful of the golden grain from the closest stalks. He began to eat the grain, discovering to his delight that the kernels had a pleasant texture and a delicious, nutty flavor. When he had eaten several handfuls, he felt a deep sense of satisfaction and wellbeing. He turned to Sir Wisdom. "I am ready," he declared, "ready to face the dragon Authades. But how do I find his hiding place?"

"Return to the scroll," the nobleman suggested with a smile, pointing to the enormous volume on the stony table.

The young prince hurried over and gazed at the silvery surface of the enormous scroll. "To find the lair of Authades," he read aloud from the open page, "follow the Path of Righteousness through the Forest of Decision."

He looked up as Sir Wisdom came up beside him. "I do not understand, sire. How can we find the lair of Authades by following the Path of Righteousness through the Forest of Decision? There seems to be no path to follow."

"Simply follow the instructions that you are given," the old man admonished, and Josiah nodded.

The young prince hesitantly crossed the clearing, walking

slowly and deliberately, for he was not at all certain that he
was heading in the right direction. To Josiah's astonishment, a
straight and narrow path appeared at his feet, visible for only
a few paces ahead of him. As he followed the path, more of
it became visible, appearing just a pace or two at a time. He
turned, searching Sir Wisdom's face for some clue that things
were amiss, but the old man followed along behind him, walking down the path as though nothing was out of the ordinary, so
Josiah continued on the unusual journey.

Prince Josiah took a deep breath. "I have a question, sire,"
he ventured. "What was the silver scroll that we saw? From
whence did it come?"

"The silver scroll is properly called the Book of Memory," Sir
Wisdom replied.

"From whence did it come, sire?"

"In reality, the Book of Memory is a collection of parchments, the sum of the passages from your book that you have
read, studied or memorized. These passages were available to
provide you guidance in your quest to find and conquer the
dragon Authades."

"How did the scroll unroll itself, sire?"

The old man smiled at this. "Did you not see the dove?"

"Nay, sire."

"The dove was opening the scroll to lead you to the appropri-
ate places in the volume," Sir Wisdom told him. "He was there
to assist you, though you did not notice him."

"Sire, look!" Prince Josiah paused in the middle of the trail
at the brink of a wide valley. On the far side of the valley, four

or five furlongs in the distance, yawned a dark opening in the side of the mountain. A cold sensation of trepidation swept over him. He knew without asking that he had reached his destination.

"The dragon's lair," he said quietly. He knew instinctively that the conflict that he was facing would change his life—for better or for worse—forever.

Chapter Nineteen

Prince Josiah and Sir Wisdom stood on the hillside above the valley, silently studying the dark opening in the mountainside opposite them. The dragon's lair was shadowy and mysterious. Sinister. A fortress of evil. Josiah swallowed hard and drew a deep breath, trying to quell the feelings of panic that threatened to overwhelm him.

"I have to confess," he told Sir Wisdom, "that at this moment my thoughts are in wild confusion. On one hand, I feel a sense of accomplishment at having found Authades' den, and I thrill with excitement as I look forward to defeating him for the honor of King Emmanuel. I am eager to return the Crown of Kuros to the control of His Majesty and thereby to know that my heart is yielded to him. But on the other hand, at this moment I am overwhelmed by feelings of fear and uncertainty. Sire, suppose that the dragon defeats and kills me, and the name of my King is thereby dishonored?"

"The battle against Authades is already won, my prince," the old man told him, glancing at the dark cavern and then back at him, "if you go trusting in Emmanuel. Use your sword and your Shield of Faith, and you shall conquer the dragon and return the crown for His Majesty's honor and glory."

Together the young prince and the old nobleman started down the hillside toward the entrance to the dragon's lair. Josiah's heart pounded with anticipation. Sir Wisdom glanced at him. "Are you not forgetting something, my prince?"

Josiah stopped in the middle of the trail. "What is that, sire?"

"Should you not send a petition to His Majesty, seeking his help in this endeavor? The dragon Authades is a powerful foe, and he seeks to destroy you. The conflict that you are facing now will be the fiercest that you have yet experienced. The name 'Josiah' means 'Emmanuel reigns', yet you dare not face Authades in your own strength. Seek the power of Emmanuel, lad, for only then shall you be victorious."

Prince Josiah nodded sheepishly. "In my zeal to slay the dragon and return the Crown of Kuros," he admitted, "I simply forgot. I am grateful that you have advised me well."

The old man smiled.

The young prince took a parchment from his book and wrote a petition to Emmanuel:

> *"To His Majesty, King Emmanuel,*
>
> *At this moment I am approaching the den of the dragon Authades that I might slay him and return the Crown of Kuros to your dominion. I humbly ask that you would grant me victory in this quest and that I might bring honor and glory to your name. I implore you, protect my heart.*
>
> *Your son, Prince Josiah"*

Josiah rolled the petition tightly, released it, and watched as it soared over the horizon on its way to the Golden City.

A sense of wellbeing swept over his soul. "What an honor," he said aloud, "to be the son of Emmanuel and therefore be allowed to send a petition to the throne room of His Majesty at any time."

Ten minutes later Prince Josiah and Sir Wisdom knelt behind a huge boulder jutting out from an expanse of sand. They cautiously studied the entrance to Authades' lair. The cavern opening loomed a mere fifty paces away, dark, sinister, and threatening. As they watched, tiny puffs of misty vapors wafted from the opening. A low hissing sound was barely audible.

Josiah nervously licked his lips and expelled his breath sharply. "I didn't realize that it was this huge," he croaked in a hoarse whisper. "The entrance must be a hundred feet high and two hundred feet wide! It looks like a gigantic mouth ready to swallow me up!"

"Now don't commence talking like that," Sir Wisdom chided. "Remember who you are! You are none other than Prince Josiah, son of His Majesty, King Emmanuel, armed with the invincible sword prepared for you by His Majesty himself.

"Authades is powerful, to be sure. As you face him you must never underestimate the vile beast's cunning, strength, or determination to destroy you. To face Authades in your own strength would be suicide. But with the mighty hand of Emmanuel upon you, you can be assured of victory. Claim the victory, my prince, in the name of His Majesty."

The young prince gulped and nodded. "I am ready, sire. Will you accompany me into the dragon's lair?"

"I was sent for that very purpose, my prince."

Josiah drew his sword. His heart was pounding as if it wanted out of his chest as he arose from his hiding place and cautiously approached the dragon's lair. Sir Wisdom was at his side.

With faltering steps the young prince entered the shadowy cavern entrance, pausing while his eyes grew accustomed to the dim light. Nervously he cleared his throat, jumping in fright as the sound echoed around the immense cavern. "What is that foul odor?" he whispered.

"That is the smell of death and decay," the old man replied quietly. "The vile creature that you are about to face has caused the demise of hundreds and hundreds before you."

"That's reassuring, sire," Josiah retorted jokingly, though he felt anything but light-hearted. He crept forward, walking noiselessly on tiptoe, completely unaware that he was doing so. His eyes were growing accustomed to the gloom and he could see that he and Sir Wisdom were standing in an immense chamber. All about him, grotesque rock formations rose from the floor like creatures from another world. He looked up. Far overhead, enormous stalactites hung from the ceiling like gigantic spears. He could only imagine what would happen if one of them should fall.

Holding his sword ready for action, the young prince turned in a slow circle, silently studying the vast cavern. Numerous openings led off from the main cavern, and Josiah realized that Authades' lair was a vast labyrinth of tunnels, passageways and chambers. *How easy it would be to get lost in here*, he thought. He crept forward, not at all certain that he was going the right way.

By now his eyes had grown accustomed to the lack of light and he made a gruesome discovery. Some of the unusual formations about him were not rock formations at all—they were piles of human bones and skulls! He shuddered.

He turned to Sir Wisdom. "Which way do I go, sire? I do not know how to find the dragon."

"Stand ready, for the dragon will find you," the old man replied. Josiah nodded and glanced around fearfully.

A hideous roar suddenly filled the cavern, so deafening and powerful that it seemed that the very mountain shook with the force of it. Josiah's heart seemed to stop. Fear tightened inside him as if he were falling through space. He dropped to his knees behind a pile of bones, eyes wide and staring, but seeing nothing. He struggled to breathe.

The dragon roared again, a prolonged burst of rage that echoed and re-echoed throughout the vast cavern until Josiah worried that his eardrums would burst with the violence of the sound. He ducked his head, gripping his helmet with both hands. His breath came in sobbing little gasps. Never before had he experienced such overwhelming, paralyzing fear.

"You are an intruder," a hissing, grating voice declared. "I know whence you have come and for what intent. Come out and show yourself, Prince Josiah! There is no hiding from me." The voice was vile, repulsive, like the oozing of putrid water, and the young prince felt fear like ice in his veins.

"Come out and show yourself!" the unseen voice demanded again. "I know where you are. There is no hiding from Authades."

The foul stench in the cavern grew stronger by the second, and Josiah realized that the dragon was approaching. His eyes frantically scanned the darkness, searching for the dragon, but he could see nothing. He cowered in fear. He heard the sound of a heavy body scraping over the stone floor of the cavern, but still could see nothing.

The young prince recoiled in fright as a hand touched his shoulder, and he barely restrained himself from crying out. He turned to look into the gentle face of Sir Wisdom. To his astonishment, the old man's face was a picture of calm assurance. "Authades is not as powerful as he wants you to think he is," he whispered. "Do not be afraid, Prince Josiah. Claim the victory over this vile monster in the name of King Emmanuel!"

Josiah swallowed hard. He opened his mouth to speak, but no sound came out. He nodded.

The old man smiled. "But remember, my prince, that you cannot fight the dragon without your sword."

In panic, Josiah looked down. His hands were empty. *Where is my sword?* he thought desperately.

Sir Wisdom was at that moment thrusting something hard and cold into his hands. "Your sword, my prince," the old man whispered with a slight smile. "You dropped it at the first roar of the dragon."

Sheepishly, the young prince accepted the weapon, wrapping his fingers around the hilt and gripping it fiercely, for his life depended upon it.

"Authades has you intimidated," the nobleman whispered, "and that's exactly what he wants. Face him, lad! Stand up to him in the name of your King! Your Shield of Faith will protect you from his fiery assaults, and your sword will pierce his scales and end his life. Go in the power of your King."

Josiah's knees were shaking as he stood to his feet. "Authades," he called, trying to keep his voice from trembling, "I have come for the Crown of Kuros! I am here in the name of His Majesty, King Emmanuel, and I lay claim to the crown for his honor and glory." He stepped from behind the pile of bones. "Return the crown to me, you vile and wretched dragon, that I may restore it to my King!"

A dark shadow moved, and Josiah realized that he was seeing the dragon for the first time. The form was indistinct and hard to make out, a dark shadow within shadows, motion without clear definition or contour. He could see that something huge was moving toward him, but could not tell of what form it was, how far away it was, or even how large it was. He waited anxiously, gripping the sword with all his might. The dragon's presence remained blurred and indistinct, like a composition of dark shadows slightly out of focus. Josiah continued to stare, trying desperately to make out the shape of his adversary, until the effort made him feel dizzy. He looked away.

The dragon spoke. "S-so, Prince Jos-s-siah," it hissed, in the hideous, grating voice that again made the young prince feel fearful, "why have you trespassed into my domain? Why have you entered my domicile? Speak, impudent prince, or I shall destroy you at once!"

"You have taken that which is not yours," Josiah challenged, taking a step toward the moving, changing image, though in truth he felt more like retreating from it. "The Crown of Kuros rightfully belongs to King Emmanuel, and I have come to re-cover it for His Majesty."

Authades roared with rage, and the cavern thundered with the echo. He moved closer, and suddenly Prince Josiah could see him clearly. The young prince gasped as he realized just how formidable an adversary he faced. The dragon was fully sixty feet long and covered from one end to the other with dull gray scales that looked as if they were made of iron. His head was immense, with huge golden eyes that smoldered with fire and a cavernous mouth with rows of wicked looking teeth. The dragon's enormous legs, sturdy as oak trees, terminated in claws that looked as if they could tear through the strongest armor. A vile stench engulfed him like a cloud.

The enormous dragon lifted his head and roared again, and for an instant, the cavern lit up like daylight as twin jets of orange flame erupted from the dragon's nostrils. "How dare you presume to enter my domain," he thundered, lashing furiously about with his tremendous scaly tail and scattering piles of bones everywhere. "Leave at once, impudent knave, or I shall destroy you here and now!"

"I come in the name of King Emmanuel," the young prince cried again, "to recover the Crown of Kuros for his honor and glory! I shall return it to the keep at the Castle of Faith where it belongs!"

The dragon laughed, a deep, rumbling chuckle that caused bursts of fire and smoke to issue from his mouth and nostrils. "Foolish prince, I have vanquished better knights than you! I have bested the Kings of the North, slain the knights from the Realm Beyond the Waters, and conquered every foe that came against me, from the Early Days until this present time. Do you not see their grinning skulls about your feet, hear their brittle bones rattling about with your every step? I can melt your armor with one breath from my mouth. I can crush you like an insect beneath my feet. My scales can turn the sharpest arrows and blunt the strongest spears. You are but a youth; I have battled for centuries. Your sword is but a needle against my tremendous strength. How dare you be so foolish as to think that you can defeat me?"

"I come in the name and the power of His Majesty," Josiah answered. "His strength is my strength."

"I shall overlook your impertinence this one time and allow you to walk out alive," Authades rumbled, stamping his mighty feet up and down as if trying desperately to control his great rage. Smoke poured from his nostrils. "Lay down your sword this instant, turn and leave my cavern, and I shall let you live to see another day. But go—go quickly—before I lose patience with you."

Prince Josiah lifted his sword and a thrill of faith swept over him. "I have come for the crown," he cried, "and I shall not leave without it!"

"Then you shall not leave at all!" Authades raged, snorting flames and smoke as he spoke. "I shall place your grinning skull beside the cavern door to greet the next foolhardy churl that ventures in to amuse me."

Josiah lifted his shield and the dragon took note. "Your puny shield and flimsy armor shall offer you no protection, foolish prince. One blast from my nostrils shall destroy your shield and armor like dry leaves thrown into a bonfire!" The dragon roared mightily and the sound reverberated within the vast cavern until the young prince thought that he not could bear another moment of the cacophony. A blast of flames exploded from the huge nostrils. "You have aroused my wrath and now you shall suffer the full fury of my vengeance. Prepare to die!"

Belching fire and smoke, Authades came thundering toward the terrified young prince with all the speed of a runaway horse. Though his heart pounded madly, Josiah stood his ground, gripping the invincible sword given him by Emmanuel. Suddenly he was engulfed in flames. The heat made him feel faint and the noxious fumes made him dizzy. And then, to his amazement, he saw that his Shield of Faith was repelling the mighty blasts from the dragon. The shield was actually deflecting the flames harmlessly away from him!

Authades attacked in fury, roaring so mightily that huge stalactites broke loose from the cavern ceiling and fell like enormous spears to the rocky floor, shattering with explosive reports. The impacts shook the vast chamber. Smoke filled the cavern as the enraged dragon snorted jets of flame from both nostrils in an attempt to scorch the young prince. Overcome with terror, Josiah lowered his sword and turned to run.

Sir Wisdom was right at his elbow. "Nay, Prince Josiah, do not flee!" he urged in a quiet but forceful voice. "Your Shield of Faith will protect you. Use your sword and slay the monster."

Heeding the nobleman's words, Prince Josiah turned back to face Authades, but at that instant the dragon's enormous head slammed into him, knocking him head over heels across the cavern. His sword clattered to the floor. Stunned, the youth lay face down upon the cold stone floor, awaiting the inevitable.

"Your sword, my prince, use your sword!" Sir Wisdom called. "The dragon is upon you, but you can defeat him with your sword!"

I have failed, the young prince thought in despair. *The dragon has won, and the Crown of Kuros will remain in his possession forever. I have failed my King.* The thought was almost more than he could bear.

Chapter Twenty

Prince Josiah lay stunned upon the cold stone floor of the dragon's lair. His sword was gone, and he knew that he was helpless against the next assault of the mighty dragon. His heart ached.

I have waited for this moment, he thought hopelessly, *dreamed of this moment when I could recover the crown for Emmanuel, and now it will never come to pass. The crown will remain forever in the clutches of this vile beast.* His head dropped, and his cheek touched the cold stone floor.

And then, determination swept across Josiah's soul like a flash of lightning. He struggled desperately to his feet. "The crown!" His cry resounded throughout the vast cavern. "The Crown of Kuros will not remain here! I shall return it to my King!" He looked around desperately. His sword lay ten feet away.

Authades saw the weapon and lunged to cut Josiah off from it. Gathering every last ounce of strength, Josiah leaped for the sword, grasping it with both hands and rolling to his feet all in one motion. The dragon collided with the young prince, his massive neck striking Josiah squarely on the shoulder and slamming him to the floor.

But the mighty sword of Emmanuel was raised the instant the dragon struck, and the invincible blade penetrated the huge reptilian scales, inflicting a terrible wound. Authades recoiled in pain, roaring hideously and retreating to a dark corner of the cavern. Josiah looked over to see small puddles of gray liquid upon the floor, and he knew that the beast was seriously wounded. Gathering his strength, he stood to his feet with renewed faith. He gripped the sword with both hands and moved forward to resume the attack.

The dragon spoke, but his tone was now subdued and conciliatory, his voice soft and appealing. "You have wounded me, stalwart prince, and we both know it. But I have also injured you. Perhaps you can manage to defeat me, but I think not. Why take this conflict any further? Why risk further harm and injury to yourself, simply to return the crown to the keeping of another? I give you my word, Prince Josiah, that I will not pursue if you will turn and walk out of this cavern. Do so now, and you shall never see me again."

"I have come for victory," Prince Josiah replied, "and I will settle for nothing less. I have come to slay you and return the crown to its rightful owner, King Emmanuel, Lord of all Terrestria."

"What will Emmanuel give you," Authades scoffed, "if you return the crown to his treasure vault? Gold? Silver? A castle of your own? I think not! Prince Josiah, I can give you wondrous things in exchange for the crown, things far grander than you could possibly dream of! I can make you wealthy, give you pleasure and prestige and power and honor, all in exchange for this trifling little crown!"

Even as the dragon spoke, enormous piles of glittering wealth appeared on the floor of the cavern. Josiah saw large wooden chests loaded with golden coins, together with heaps of silver ingots, diamonds, emeralds and rubies. Rich and costly clothing, prancing, well-bred horses, castles and lands and beautiful women and ornate swords and exquisitely tooled armor—the finest that Terrestria had to offer was paraded before his eyes in a moment of time.

"This is yours, all yours, in exchange for the Crown of Kuros," the dragon offered. "Will Emmanuel give you as much for placing the crown within his dominion?"

"The Crown of Kuros belongs to His Majesty, King Emmanuel, and I will not rest until I have returned it to his possession!" the young prince cried, striding forward to engage the dragon again. "The crown will be returned to the keep at the Castle of Faith before another sunset takes place!"

"Spare me, but take the crown," the dragon bargained, still speaking from the dark recesses of the cave where Josiah could not see him. "I shall yield the crown on the condition that you will not seek to destroy me."

"He is attempting to set a snare for you," Sir Wisdom warned in a quiet voice, and Josiah looked around to see that the old man was at his side. "Accept no concessions and strike no deals with this vile creature. Your King would have you utterly destroy the dragon."

Josiah nodded to show that he understood.

"What will it be, valiant prince?" the dragon queried, still out of sight in the shadows. "Will you accept the Crown of Kuros in return for the sparing of my life?"

"I have come to slay you and I will make no concessions!" the young prince cried, running toward the darkness with which the dragon shrouded himself.

"Then this battle is to the death!" Authades roared. "I warn you, insolent prince, that in wounding me, you wound yourself. My pain will be your pain. Should you prevail and somehow slay me, you would slay a part of yourself. Do you still desire to destroy me, knowing that it will cost you?"

Prince Josiah simply did not reply. Lifting his sword, he leaped toward the shadows.

An enormous yellow reptilian head with black death markings rose to meet his charge. The huge mouth opened in a hiss of fury, revealing fangs fully two feet long that dripped with transparent yellow venom. Josiah stopped short, and his breath caught in his throat. He had seen this creature before. Leaping to one side, he rolled behind a formation of rock.

"The Serpent of Selfishness!" he whispered in amazement to Sir Wisdom, as his companion joined him behind the rock. "The dragon Authades is in reality the Serpent of Selfishness! I have battled this serpent before."

"Selfishness takes many forms," the old man said, with a nod of agreement. "You now know how the enchantress Morphina was able to assume such a variety of appearances so rapidly."

Josiah stared at him as a sudden realization dawned. "Morphina was the Serpent of Selfishness!" he said aloud. "The enchantress, the dragon, and the serpent are one and the same!"

"You now know your adversary," Sir Wisdom replied. "And you now know why you can never accept any concessions or strike any deals with this vile creature. The serpent must be destroyed, or the Crown of Kuros will never reach the King's treasure vault. But use caution, Prince Josiah, for the serpent's fangs carry a deadly poison that will enter your heart and cause you to lose interest in serving your King or returning the Crown of Kuros to the keep."

"If the crown never reaches the keep, my heart will never be completely yielded, and I desire that more than life itself," the young prince declared. "With the help of His Majesty, I will destroy the serpent ere I leave this cavern."

The serpent struck at that moment, drawing his head fully twenty feet above the cavern floor and then slashing downward like a bolt of lightning. Josiah leaped backward and the deadly fangs missed his legs by less than a foot. Hissing angrily, the murderous reptile struck a second time, again with the speed of lightning. Josiah anticipated the strike and managed to roll behind a huge boulder just in time. His heart trembled when he saw huge coils of pale yellow reptilian flesh gliding noiselessly through the piles of bones as the giant snake moved closer and gathered himself for yet another strike.

"Stand up to him, my prince!" Sir Wisdom called. "Use your sword!"

The huge head rose high in the air above the rock behind which Josiah was crouching. The enormous tongue darted in and out as the snake scented the air; huge, golden reptilian eyes scanned the cavern—the snake was searching for him. The enormous fangs were wet and glistening and dripping a clear yellow liquid. Josiah shuddered, knowing that he was seeing the poison that could take his life.

The Serpent of Selfishness struck again at that instant, but the young prince was ready for him. As the gigantic head swept downward, Josiah swung the mighty sword with all of his strength. Steel penetrated reptilian flesh. Hissing angrily, the giant snake recoiled. The fearsome head disappeared from sight behind a small mountain of bones.

Spotting a thick coil of pale yellow between two rocky formations, Josiah sprang forward and hacked at it with all his might. A hideous roar echoed through the vast cavern and the yellow coil disappeared from sight. Josiah knew that he had inflicted a serious wound. He turned and dashed across the cavern and ducked into the shadows behind a pile of bones.

"Prince Josiah! Beware!"

Josiah turned just as the huge head crashed down from the shadows. Swinging his sword to defend himself, he leaped backward with all his might. The deadly fangs missed him by inches, but the glittering blade of his sword struck home, once again wounding the Serpent of Selfishness. The fearsome head swept upward and disappeared as quickly as it had come.

Gripping the sword with both hands, Josiah stood poised for another attack. He listened intently, but heard nothing. The cavern was silent, deathly silent, as if time itself was waiting with bated breath for the outcome of the fierce conflict. Josiah's heart pounded.

He sensed rather than heard movement behind him. Spinning around, he caught sight of the golden, malevolent eyes and the deadly fangs as they drew back into the shadows of a narrow passageway. The serpent was watching him, watching and waiting for the opportunity for another strike.

The young prince ventured out into the open. The Serpent of Selfishness struck in fury with a roaring hiss that reverberated through the entire cavern. Two deadly fangs loaded with lethal venom slashed downward. Josiah stood his ground, thrusting upwards with all his might at the giant reptilian head. The invincible blade pierced the snake's mouth between the two fangs, and the Serpent of Selfishness jerked back. He struck again and again, one lightning-quick strike after another in quick succession, but each time Josiah met the deadly strikes with steel. The serpent slowly withdrew, and Josiah's heart leaped. He had won the battle!

The young prince stepped back and dropped the point of his sword to the earth, resting both hands upon the hilt as he caught his breath and watched the colossal reptile retreat.

"Prince Josiah, beware!" Sir Wisdom's warning came just in time. Josiah spun around just as a huge, scaly head rose menacingly above him. The serpent had disappeared, and once again, the young prince found that he was battling the dragon Authades. The dragon's tail whipped through the air, knocking Josiah off his feet and causing him to drop his sword.

Josiah lunged forward with all his strength and managed to grasp the sword with one hand. Rolling over on his side, he leaped to his feet again just as a withering blast of flame erupted from the dragon's mouth. Deflecting the fiery assault with his Shield of Faith, Josiah thrust upward with all his strength, driving the blade of his mighty sword through the reptile's head. The dragon Authades sagged to the floor of his own cavern, trembling and crying so terribly that the cavern rang with the sound. His tail thrashed from side to side, scattering bones about the vast chamber. He raised his head and breathed one final snort of flame, and then with a shudder, lay still, defeated and lifeless. Josiah's mighty shout of victory echoed throughout the vast chamber.

Prince Josiah stood twenty paces from the lifeless dragon, silently surveying the enormous carcass. He lowered the point of his sword until it touched the stony floor. Victory was his, and yet he felt no surge of elation or pride. His heart swelled with gratitude as he realized how vastly different the outcome could have been. Sir Wisdom appeared at his elbow. "There were two times, sire," the young prince said in a quiet voice, "that I thought that surely I had been defeated and the dragon had won the conflict. I almost despaired of recovering the Crown of Kuros for His Majesty."

He suddenly glanced around the vast cavern. "Where is the crown, anyway? I have not yet seen it, nor do I know how to find it."

"My prince," the old man said softly, pointing at the giant carcass, "behold!"

As Josiah watched in horrified fascination, the dragon's scales slowly turned a horrid shade of green. One by one they began to fall off, dropping to the stone floor with tinkling sounds and shattering into tiny fragments as if made of glass. Within moments, the gigantic carcass was completely stripped of its scales. The body began to disintegrate, collapsing upon itself and melting away into a sticky puddle of slime. A puff of smoke appeared, and then a thick cloud of smoke billowed upward from the puddle. When the smoke cleared there was nothing left but a dark stain upon the stone floor. The young prince stepped closer. "Not much remains of the mighty Authades," he remarked, suddenly experiencing a refreshing sense of relief. "He shall trouble me no more."

As he spoke, a tiny sparkle of light from the dark floor caught his eye. Stepping over, he looked closer. Lying at his feet was a wondrous, glittering crown—a small, transparent crown with a base of solid gold. He stooped and reverently picked it up.

"The Crown of Kuros!" he said in awe. "Authades had it with him! As of this moment, it is now under the authority of His Majesty, King Emmanuel, for my heart is now yielded and I am under Emmanuel's command."

He turned toward his companion. "Somehow I thought that the crown would be larger, sire," he said softly. "It barely fills my hand."

"The crown was fashioned from a single, flawless diamond," the old man replied. "Though it is not large, its value is immense; and its significance is even greater." He put a gentle hand on the youth's shoulder. "Shall we journey to the Castle of Faith?"

Prince Josiah reverently raised the Crown of Kuros with both hands. "My Lord, my King, the crown belongs to you and you alone! Emmanuel, my King, my heart is yours!"

A song of praise and gratitude burst from Prince Josiah's lips as he and Sir Wisdom walked from the gloom of the cavern into the brilliant afternoon sunshine.

Glossary

Bailey: the courtyard in a castle.

Barbican: the space or courtyard between the inner and outer walls of a castle.

Battlement: on castle walls, a parapet with openings behind which archers would shelter when defending the castle.

Castle: a fortified building or complex of buildings, used both for defense and as the residence for the lord of the surrounding land.

Coat of arms: an arrangement of heraldic emblems, usually depicted on a shield or standard, indicating ancestry and position.

Curtain: the protective wall of a castle.

Daub-and-wattle: type of wall construction in which a latticework of wood or reeds is filled in with mud or plaster.

Doublet: a close-fitting garment worn by men.

Ewer: a pitcher with a wide spout.

Fletching: feathers at the rear end of an arrow that help provide accuracy in shooting.

Furlong: a measurement of distance equal to one-eighth of a mile.

Garrison: a group of soldiers stationed in a castle.

Gatehouse: a fortified structure built over the gateway to a castle.

Great hall: the room in a castle where the meals were served and the main events of the day occurred.

Greave: piece of armor protecting the leg below the knee.

Jerkin: a close-fitting jacket or short coat.

Keep: the main tower or building of a castle.

Lance: a thrusting weapon with a long wooden shaft and a sharp metal point.

Longbow: a hand-drawn wooden bow $5\frac{1}{2}$ to 6 feet tall.

Lute: a stringed musical instrument having a long, fretted neck and a hollow, pear-shaped body.

Lyre: a musical instrument consisting of a sound box with two curving arms carrying a cross bar from which strings are stretched to the sound box.

Minstrel: a traveling entertainer who sang and recited poetry.

Moat: a deep, wide ditch surrounding a castle, often filled with water.

Portcullis: a heavy wooden grating covered with iron and suspended on chains above the gateway or any doorway of a castle. The portcullis could be lowered quickly to seal off an entrance if the castle was attacked.

Reeve: an appointed official responsible for the security and welfare of a town or region.

Saboton: pointed shoes made of steel to protect the feet of a knight in battle.

Salet: a protective helmet usually made of steel, worn by knights in combat.

Scullion: a kitchen servant who is assigned menial work

Sentry walk: a platform or walkway around the inside top of a castle curtain used by guards, lookouts and archers defending a castle.

Solar: a private sitting room or bedroom designated for royalty or nobility.

Standard: a long, tapering flag or ensign, as of a king or a nation.

Stone: a British unit of weight equal to fourteen pounds.

Tunic: a loose-fitting, long-sleeved garment.

Trencher: a flat piece of bread on which meat or other food was served.

Castle Facts

- A knight's sword weighed about $2\frac{1}{2}$ pounds.

- The castle well was usually inside the castle walls so that the castle inhabitants would still have access to it in the event of a siege.

- Often an attacking commander would attempt to bribe a castle resident to poison the well.

- Rounded towers and walls could withstand battering rams and missiles better than angled ones.

- Large castles often had their own fishponds, orchards and vineyards.

- At the age of seven, a boy could become a page and begin training in riding and sword fighting.

- At the age of fourteen, a page became a knight's esquire, looking after his lord's horses and armor.

- Most esquires had become knights by the time they were twenty-one years old.